D0104803

PROJECT

NIMROD

ANADIA DARDEN

To every brown boy in the entire world. You are
appreciated, you are valued, you are loved.
Your story matters.

A special shoutout to my three brown boys and their dad:
Tremmell, JT, iNDy, and Tripp. You helped me find my
voice. Every word I ever write is yours.

To everyone not mentioned:
Calm down. I will write more books, I promise. My only
motivation to write more books is to dedicate them to all of
you. I'm sure this fact will go over well with my therapist
(who will also have a book dedication).

Acknowledgments

I've always been extremely confident while deathly afraid of failure... but God. Praise Him high, praise Him low. I have been blessed with an amazing circle that has seen me through all my procrastination, fear, and doubt. I will spend my life making sure they know how loved and appreciated they are.

My parents who shaped, pushed, and prodded: Mommy, Daddy, and Erica. There's no rhyme or reason to why you love me like you, why you love my children like your own, why you've poured all of you into me without ever thinking twice. There's no question that I owe you everything and I know you'll never let me repay you. There's no question that I am who I am because you loved me. You all know how important you are to me. I tell you all the time. Thank you.

My awesome siblings, my inspirations who keep me young-ish: Nika, Aaron, Aerick, and Attahlah: You have my heart. Always have, always will.

Grandmother and Auntie, my boos: You just don't know... you couldn't possibly. I don't even have the words.

I love you, I just love you both so much it doesn't make sense.

My tribe who has had my back since the 7th grade. Who always believed and always held me accountable: Thank you. I love you, Michelle and Kourtney.

Uncle Jim: You welcomed me with open arms and endless support. You are such an integral piece of my puzzle. I pray you know that.

The talented digital artist who created my illustrations, Daniel K.D. : Thank you so much!

Chynna Denny, publisher extraordinaire: Hunter would not have a physical home without you. Thank you, thank you, thank you.

To my incredible editor, Laci Swann: Thank you for your patience and encouragement. You're stuck with me until I forget words exist. You'll deal.

My phenomenally supportive family: My boys, my muses, my reasons. I love you more than words can ever express. My super-human husband who always stayed positive and always reminded me of my worth, always... Did I say always? My biggest fan, my only fan. Your drive encourages me, your faith keeps me centered. Forever my Neo. I just love you, okay?

Chapter One

"Hunter! Lights *off*," Mom screamed up the stairs.

Silly me. There I was, under the impression that middle school would usher in a new sleep schedule. I guess not.

Sure, I was tired. I didn't have breakfast this morning because I overslept, so I struggled through my first two periods.

My stomach growled so angrily that the girl sitting next to me stared in bewilderment and asked if I was okay. I wasn't really embarrassed because she's a bit of a bookworm. I'm sure she was actually concerned and not secretly looking for an angle to crack a joke. I politely shrugged her off. I'm a skinny kid. Algebra was not the place to discuss weight class.

After school, I had Math Club, but before you think I'm an academic scholar of some sort, Math Club is just the name they gave tutoring so that we don't feel too dumb. Math used to be easy… well, easier, but in my humble opinion, numbers just don't make sense when you complicate things by adding letters.

I'd once asked in class, "Are we learning math or language? Make up your mind!"

I got in trouble for that. Mr. Lawson wrote a nicely worded email to my mother that more or less read: Your kid is an M-O-R-O-N (smiley face).

All in all, I didn't really care what they called it because the truth of the matter was, I needed help. My low "C" was dropping by the day, and I had to earn all As, Bs, and Cs to stay off of punishment and on the basketball team. The threat of a "D" was looming, and that meant not only basketball, but my video games were on the line. I was terrified.

That day, Math Club crawled along like a lazy snail, and the one-hour session felt more like three. I think I might have actually fallen asleep a few times. X and Y-intercepts simply weren't enough to keep me awake through my hunger and physical fatigue. It didn't help that I had given my lunch to my friend Brooke, so I was absolutely famished.

I saw her standing in the caf, looking confused and angry, and I was compelled to ask her what was wrong. Normally, 7th grade girls don't really talk much to 7th grade boys, but our mothers work together, so we've known one another since the second grade. I walked across the cafeteria with my chest out like a knight, ready to rescue his damsel.

"Brooke, what's the matter?" I asked.

"Dom is a jerk, and I hate him," she sighed.

Before I had a chance to ask what her idiot older brother had done, she was staring up at me with puppy dog eyes. Unbeknownst to her, the puppy dog eyes were completely unnecessary; she could have the shirt off my back if she asked.

"Can I borrow five bucks? He took my lunch money this morning and I'm totally starving."

Not quite what I expected.

"Sure," I said.

I was hungry, but what was I supposed to do? Let the most popular girl in school starve? I wasn't ready to commit social suicide. But the thing was, I was broke.

"I don't have any money on me, but you can have my lunch," I replied as I handed her the brown paper bag from my backpack.

This wasn't easy for me because it was my absolute favorite – lasagna – but, anything for Brooke.

I wanted her to know how much of a big deal it was to give her my lasagna. How much it pained me to hand it over, but I don't think she picked up on that. I don't even think she ate it. In fact, I'm pretty sure I saw her throw it away as I walked out of the cafeteria.

My dad always says, "Everybody plays the fool sometimes." Well, I'm a fool for her *all the time*.

He also says that the nice guy always wins, so maybe I'm in there? Either way, I was still hungry and a little crushed with most of the day still ahead of me.

By the time I walked home after tutoring, basketball practice, and homework, all I wanted to do was sit on the couch and watch tv, but alas, I had chores: wash the dishes, sweep the kitchen, and walk the dog.

After dinner, I hopped in the shower, washed up, and collapsed on the couch in the loft. The movie channel was calling my name.

I didn't even get a chance to skip the intro to episode five of my favorite show before Mom screamed for me to go to bed. I'll be 14 on my next birthday, did she seriously think ten o'clock was a suitable time to go to bed?

I decided it was time we reached a new agreement.

I would have to watch my words and my tone as I approached my parents to renegotiate, so I practiced a bit before approaching them.

"'Mom, Cadence goes to bed at nine-thirty, and she's eight. No way that's fair!'"

"Fair!?" I could already hear her reply. Let's start over.

"Mom, I work really hard at school and practice, and then I come home and work hard on my chores. I think I deserve an extra hour!"

"You work hard?! You deserve?!" she'd say incredulously.

I needed to change my approach.

"*Dad*, I'd like to stay up a little later to go over game plays and footage. I'd also like to stay up to watch some NBA games if that's okay with you guys."

Ding, ding, ding. We've got a winner!

Dealing with parents is a science that I've happened to master.

I slowly crept downstairs, gauging the room before submitting my case. Mom was giggling, and Dad was whispering in her ear – gross, but good for my chances.

I stated my case with confidence and humility.

I listened patiently without interruption or rebuttal as my parents discussed the matter brought before them.

Lights off at 11!

Hook, line, and sinker. A win for 13-year-olds across the globe. You're welcome.

With my extra hour secured, I ran up the stairs to finish my show. But after ten minutes, the show was watching me. I know, I know, but in my defense, I was exhausted. Besides, it's my time. I fought for it and could do whatever I wanted with it, and at that moment, I wanted to sleep.

***

I welcomed sleep and fully embraced its warm hold, but I was met with its cold, wet snout.

I had only been asleep for about 20 minutes when our ancient cocker spaniel, Callie, decided to cover me with love, and by love, I mean her incredibly wet tongue.

It took me a second to wake up and gather my thoughts.

Where am I?

What's going on?

Oh yeah; loft, couch, television. Got it.

I tried to stand up to get in bed, but my legs rebelled, so I plopped back onto the couch. I guess I'm staying put. I don't mind sleeping on the couch anyway, it means I don't have to make my bed in the morning.

Something's off, I thought to myself as I was smacked in the face with a whiff of a horrible, nostril-flaring stench right below my head. Hesitantly, I glanced to the floor - first, let me reiterate just how ancient Callie is: She was my Granma Lou's dog. Mom found her in a shelter and knew she would be a great friend for Granma, who had been lonely since Papa died. Mom was right. Granma and Callie were inseparable. A while ago, I regretfully walked in on them showering together. I shudder at the memory. I love Callie for bringing joy back to my Granma's eyes for the brief time she was still with us.

Unfortunately, we lost her to breast cancer last year. I miss her a lot. She was old, but we were friends. Granma Lou was so funny, and she cursed a lot. She was honest and loving, and I told her secrets all the time because she was on my side, not Mom and Dad's. Sometimes, I still tell her my secrets. I keep that from Mom because I know she misses Granma way more than me.

I was starting to get emotional, until my stomach turned a bit.

Yep, our 16-year-old cocker spaniel was reverting to infancy and had pooped on the rug just like a puppy. She's super old, 87 in dog years and I know when you're old, you need diapers.

I wouldn't have minded it so much, except... I think she was licking it.

No way.

She wasn't.

She wouldn't.

Oh, but she was – she's eating it!

Suddenly, I was fully awake and aware – she was just licking my face! I screamed and ran to the bathroom.

Callie had just feasted on her own poop and proceeded to lick my face. I was completely and utterly disgusted. I had to shower, brush my teeth... something.

I slammed the bathroom door behind me and started to take off my clothes. I grabbed my toothbrush, smothered it in toothpaste, and scrubbed my teeth. I had to get the dog poop stench out of my nostrils. Yes, I realized neither my teeth nor my mouth had anything to do with Callie licking my cheek, but being minty fresh never hurt anyone, and I needed to be as fresh as possible.

My parents, having heard my blood-curdling scream, ran to find me. Worried and completely oblivious to the fact that I was totally naked, they burst through the bathroom door.

"What happened? Are you okay?" Mom shrieked. My mom's worry sensor is permanently set to sensitive. She's overly concerned with mine and Cadence's safety. I'm surprised she even lets us go to school.

I covered myself with the decorative towel hanging behind the sink. "I'm fine. Can you guys please get out?!"

"First of all, I made you. You were completely naked when you came out of my stomach. Secondly, I don't know how many times I've told you not to touch those towels! They're made to look at, not use, especially not by a stinky teenager."

Dad walked away as soon as he realized there was no imminent danger. He didn't care about decorative towels or nudity. He just wanted to get back to his spot on the couch and the game. He tried to drag Mom away with him, but she started going off on a tangent about how I don't listen and that she's never going to visit my smelly, non-existent apartment. She always goes straight to teenage funk. I didn't think I smelled that bad. I remembered to put on deodorant almost every day. She's also taken this opportunity to straighten my bathroom.

"Hello, Lady!!" I wanted to scream. "I'm standing here nearly naked. Can you let go of your fixation with towels?!"

Instead, I simply stated, "Mom, Callie pooped in the loft."

I could barely get the words out before she shouted down the stairs for my dad to get the carpet cleaner.

I was tired of everything and everyone. I washed my face and climbed in bed, ready for the day to be over.

Chapter Two

You know that weird feeling you get when someone's watching you? I sometimes get a feeling like that when someone's talking about me; at least that's what I think is happening when someone randomly pops into my mind.

The next morning, while toasting my waffles, a thought of Brian, our old neighbor, entered my brain. Brian was a few years older than me, so I never got to know him well, but he was always nice to Cadence and me. He would play basketball with me all afternoon, which, when I think of it, was really an act of kindness because I sucked until last year when I started playing more.

Brian never let me win, but he didn't destroy me, either. Cool guy. I wondered how he was doing.

"Have you talked to Brian's mom?" I asked Mom, searching her expressionless face to see if she was listening. She wasn't. She was watching Cadence make a mess attempting to cut her French toast.

"Mom," I implored. She snapped out of it but stayed trained on Cadence.

"No, I haven't," she replied. "I haven't spoken to her since they put their house on the market. I did see Brian on the news the other day, though. Apparently, he broke some shooting record over at Shadow Ridge. Maybe I'll call her today… Cay, do you want me to help you?"

"I got it," Cadence insisted as she made a complete mess.

Mom complained, "Then can you do it like I showed you? You're just ripping it apart."

"It's all going in my tummy. It doesn't have to be pretty," Cadence asserted boldly.

Shocked, I sat back and waited to see how this would pan out. Cay is feisty. I've heard Mom say that she loves and loathes this part of her personality. She said that she wants her to be strong and assertive but also respectful and considerate.

I suppose what parents want from their children differs per kid because I feel like I'm all of those things and a little extra wrapped in this lanky 5'9" frame, but she doesn't see me that way.

Mom thinks I'm manipulative while I see myself as calculated. I prefer to map out my steps to elicit a particular response. Eh, tomato, tomahto.

"Watch it, Cadence," Mom warned as she shot her only daughter severe eye darts.

That was all Cadence needed to hear to straighten up and fly right. She was feisty, but she didn't want to get on Mom's bad side she wasn't dumb. None of us wanted to get on Mom's bad side, not even Dad. Cay sat upright in her chair and was deliberate in arranging the pieces of her French toast. Mom was satisfied, but I knew she was being a smart aleck. I chuckled. Cadence giggled. Mom smiled.

I love them. They're crazy, but I love them.

"Hunt, do you want a ride to school this morning?" Mom probed. "Cay is riding with Emily.

You wouldn't let me make you breakfast. Let me drop you off."

I responded a little too quickly. "I'm going to see if Dom and B can pick me up."

She snickered. "Oh. Dom and '*B*,' huh? Okay, let me know how that goes."

I shot her an exasperated glance. She's so annoying.

One day, she found a letter I wrote Brooke, and she's been extra cheesy ever since. I had no intentions of giving Brooke the letter. It's just easier to talk to paper, which is weird because we've known each other almost our whole lives. I don't know why I get so nervous around her. I wonder if she can tell.

I grabbed my phone and called Dominic. It rang a few times before he picked up.

"Hunt, what's up?" he answered.

"Have you left your house yet? Can you come get me on your way to drop Brooke off?"

"You forgot to say the magic word," he teased. I was almost positive he was about to say "no" and found satisfaction in making me grovel.

"Please," I mumbled reluctantly.

He responded, "I'm actually outside of your house right now."

I ran to the window in the living room. What? Why was he here? I hung up the call and ran outside.

"What's up, loser?" I heard him call out as I opened the door.

I scanned the car—no Brooke. However, Brian was in the passenger seat.

"Hey, Brian," I exclaimed, ignoring Dom. "I just asked my mom about you this morning. She said you broke some record. Congratulations."

"It's nothing," he remarked humbly as he reached out to slap my hand.

Dominic interrupted, "Uh, hello! I'm here."

"My bad. Hey, Dom. What are you doing here? Where's Brooke?" I asked inquisitively.

He adjusted his rearview mirror and played with his phone, "She went early for some meeting. My dad dropped her off, but she told me you gave her your lunch yesterday, so I wanted to give you the five bucks I took from her. I never needed it. When I asked her what she had for lunch, she told me what you did. I was going to give her the money back, but she doesn't deserve it. She's a mean girl. Do you know she didn't even eat it? Ugh, she gets on my nerves. Anyway, you want a ride or what?"

I stood there in shock. B, a mean girl? Dom, a nice guy? What's going on here?

"Hunt?!" Dom reeled me back in. "We don't have all day. Get in," he exclaimed as he threw the door to the back seat open. I hopped in, empty-handed. He pulled away as I realized I had absolutely nothing other than my phone. No backpack, no laptop, nothing I needed to have a productive day.

Dom's car looked like it had been hit by a tornado. Books, papers, water bottles, and balls from just about every sport covered the floor and seats. There was also a wide array of crumbs and leftovers. I swore I saw a whole hotdog without a bun under a failed trigonometry test. I tucked my hand in my sleeve and brushed the debris from my body.

"Do you *ever* clean this car?" I asked. I felt as if he could very well answer "no."

His voice reeked of irritation. "Don't like it, get out and walk. I'm doing you a favor. Never bite the hand that feeds you."

Silently, I took my phone from my pocket and texted Mom. Hopefully, she would meet me at school. I needed my laptop for first period.

Dom drives like a madman, so I made sure to buckle my seatbelt. I double and triple checked that it was secure... this could get ugly.

Lawrence STEM Academy is about five minutes from my house, but we had to pass an elementary school to get there, and the speed limit drops to 15 miles per hour. Dom's reputation clearly preceded him because the crossing guards eyed him as they shielded the tiny school-goers. I wondered what he could have possibly done to make those sweet old ladies so aggravated.

I didn't have to wonder long as Dom cranked his radio to obnoxious levels and stared one woman directly in the eye.

Lil Yachty chastised her: *"Diamond in the rough, you look as good as Oprah's bank account."*

I put my face in my hands. I was so embarrassed for him. Thankfully, Brian brought our stalemate to an end, turning the music down to zero.

"Bro, are you crazy? Would you do your grandmother like that?"

Dom's response was typical. "My grandmother wouldn't be out here helping little kids cross the street. She's at home watching Oprah like these old ladies should be doing. I'm simply reminding them that Oprah's on."

"I swear, I don't know why I hang out with you," Brian said.

"Because I get money *and* girls. Imagine being as lit as me," Dom exclaimed.

Laughing, Brian quipped, "All I know is I better not ever hear of you disrespecting my grandmother out here."

I barely heard them. I was back in Granma Lou's Buick, rapping Drake lyrics. She knew every word to "God's Plan." I once asked her how she learned the lyrics. Apparently, she asked Alexa to play some gospel song, and she got Drake instead. She said she didn't care for the "yucky words," but she was happy that Drake kept God relevant to my generation. I think she added the part about cursing just for me because she always rapped the bad words aggressively.

I smiled.

We sped off, all but burning rubber. I decided never to ride with Dom again.

I saw LMS about a block away. I had never been more thankful to see my school in my life. Before throwing me out of the car, Dom shoved a five in my hand and apologized again. I guess, deep down, he really is a nice guy… deep, deep down. I rushed a quick "bye" to Brian, but he was fully engulfed in a text message. I don't even think he heard me.

Unlike Dom, I really looked up to Brian. He was nice, smart, and a certified bucket. It also helped that he was only in the 10th grade. He would be a senior when I finally got to Shadow Ridge. I was really hoping to make varsity as a freshman so that we could play together, but first, I had to get through 7th-grade math. *Ugh.*

Chapter Three

We pulled up to the school's back entrance where all the popular girls hang before the bell rings. I scored a few cool points having Dom drop me off, which was cool since all the middle school girls love high school boys.

I was a little nervous because boys usually go in through the yard. I figured all eyes would be on me, and I was right. They started whispering as soon as I stepped out of the backseat. Apparently, they didn't mind the candy wrappers and crumbs that fell out with me.

Sidebar: Mom always tells me to keep my room clean because girls don't like boys with dirty rooms or stinky pits. That was obviously a lie. Girls like cool boys, even if they stink (which again, I do not) or have dirty cars.

Anyway, they had all seen Dom dropping Brooke off, but me getting out of the car was a surprise they'd be talking about all day. I was uneasy with the thought of them gossiping about me. I've heard the way they pick boys apart. I was a fairly popular guy, and I wanted it to stay that way. I couldn't take any hits to my reputation, not if I ever expected to date Brooke.

Until recently, I hadn't wanted to date anyone. I enjoyed being a "bachelor." That changed the day I overheard a bunch of girls saying that Brooke liked me. Nothing has been the same since that fateful day. Every move I made has been calculated – my clothes and haircut had to be fresh, I started wearing cologne, and I begged mom to let me get my ears pierced. Her response was brutal. I don't want to relive that.

I don't know why, but it seemed that the harder I tried, the *less* attention she paid me. Today was different, though, everyone was watching, and I knew she would hear about it.

I walked past the lip-glossed whisperers, trying not to look at anyone, giving them a quick nod without a single word. This might've been the coolest thing I ever did. I was almost inside the gate, almost solidified into the LMS hall of fame, when I heard it... her... *I heard my mom.*

"Hunter. Hunter, baby! Mommy's here," she shouted... and she would not stop.

I ignored her. I had no other choice. I just kept walking. I hurried my steps as the murmurs got louder.

"Whose mom is that?"

"I'd die if my mom..."

The worst was the mocking.

"Baby, baby..."

Ugh, I hate teenagers.

You don't know my mom. Yes, she's extremely overprotective and overly concerned with decorative towels, but she is also the nicest mean person you'll ever meet. Take today, for instance – she brought my backpack to school, nice. But she embarrassed me, and I'm fairly sure it was on purpose, mean. She's like a little fruity Sour Patch Kid – sweet but very much sour. Not to mention, I was definitely going to get in trouble for ignoring her... big trouble.

"I know you hear me, Hunter Daniel Stevens," she called.

All three names?

Make that very big trouble.

I was in for it, so I figured I might as well go for the gusto: I ran away as fast as I could. Never had I been more appreciative of the school's policy of no visitors on campus, which ensured she could not follow me.

I was early for first period, which was STEM. Thankful for the time to catch my breath, I sat at my desk and put my head down. I reached down to get my water bottle from my backpack and remembered my bag wasn't there. As I sulked in my parched disappointment, Mrs. Lattimore from the front office walked into the room. I was a student aide the previous semester, so I knew that Mrs. Lattimore came to "fetch" students whose parents dropped something off before classes started for the day. During class, aides got to run around campus delivering backpacks, lunches, and whatnot. I stood because I knew she was there for me.

"Stevens," Mr. Hill bellowed without looking up from his playbook to see me already heading in his direction. I walked out of the door without acknowledging his summons. He wasn't paying attention anyway. In addition to being the STEM teacher, Mr. Hill was our basketball coach. I honestly preferred him as a tech nerd than a coach.

I beat Mrs. Lattimore to the office. I wanted to grab my backpack and dip. I went directly to the desk, where she kept students' belongings, but again, much to my dismay, there was no bag. Now, I would have to wait for her to get back. This could take a while, considering her 80-something-year-old legs didn't move with any urgency.

I sighed and flopped into the chair at the empty desk when none other than Brooke walked past.

"Hey, Hunt," she said cheerfully. "I heard Ms. Alex was looking for you earlier. What was that about?"

Of course *that's* what she heard about.

Nervously, I responded, "She came to drop off my backpack, and apparently, to embarrass me."

"I love her. She's so funny. I bet she was calling you 'Baby,' huh?"

"You already know. She's such a bot. I ran from her."

In complete shock, Brooke responded, "You ran from who?!"

"I know I'm in trouble. I can kiss my phone goodbye and probably the PS4. She used all three of my names," I said, lowering my voice to whisper the part about my names.

B knows my middle name, but that's not the kind of information you want floating around school. It's crazy that you have to guard your personal information like a squirrel guards an acorn, but kids at my school will make fun of you for anything, and I mean *anything*.

"Dang, Daniel," she laughed as she turned to walk to class. While the pop culture reference is not lost through her G-rated office-talk, I give her a sarcastic laugh. First, because that's old. No one says it anymore. Second, her knowing and openly sharing my middle name is the exact reason no one here really knows me. They use everything against you.

Moments later, in walked Mrs. Lattimore with my backpack on her shoulder.

"Mr. Stevens," she screeched. "I call myself being nice and bringing your bag to you this morning. I trekked through the Blue and Orange buildings with this monstrous sack on my back, doing you a favor, and you completely ignored me when I got to your class! That's not the Hunter I know. What's gotten into you? And what have you got in this bag?!"

"Oh, my goodness, Mrs. L. I'm so sorry. It's been a rough morning, and I didn't want to miss any class instruction," I lied. "So, I was hurrying to get here, grab my bag, and get back to class."

It wasn't a complete lie. I wanted to grab my bag and get out of the office quickly, but not to rush back to class. I planned on making a pit stop in the bathroom to check Snap. Surely, there were several snaps of my mom. I needed to assess the damage.

I ran to Mrs. Lattimore and relieved the burden on her aged back.

"I didn't mean for you to have to lug my backpack around. After school, I have basketball practice, so my shoes, practice uniform, and water bottle are in there. Sheesh, I'm sorry, ma'am."

I truly felt bad. Mrs. L, as I lovingly coined her, is the sweetest lady on campus. The lunch ladies are cool, too, they give you extra food if you keep the caf in order and make sure everyone picks up after themselves. But no one is Mrs. Lattimore, not even close. I don't know why I took such a liking to an old woman, but I did.

"I'm sure you didn't, but my feelings are still hurt," she scoffed. "Now hurry back to class. I don't want you to see me cry."

She sent me on my way with a wink. She's so sweet. She reminds me of a lot of Granma.

Chapter Four

Every class before lunch seemed to fly by with DSL speed. Why is time so fickle? Neither doodling, nor napping... not even actually paying attention to the teacher made time speed by like this.

I desperately needed more time to regroup, to get my mind right for whatever was waiting for me at lunch. There was still a chance that everyone forgot about my mother's special appearance, I kept my fingers, legs, and eyes crossed.

I snuck to the bathroom before going back to class to check Snap, and there wasn't one story featuring my mom. I was relieved but cautious.

It seemed the day was back on track. I got a lot of texts about this morning's grand entrance. I tried to play it cool and left everyone on read. My plan was to act like I didn't care—the more nonchalant, the better.

At lunch, no one mentioned my mom. For once, it seemed that this unforgiving school decided to cut me some slack.

Since I had an extra five bucks, I decided to get pizza for lunch. My friend, Jude, was at the front of the line, talking to his little brother. I slid in front of him, cutting about 15 people. I put my hands together in a praying motion, thanking everyone I cut for being cool. Some shot me dirty looks while most weren't paying attention. The nerdy girl from math, Jenn, was three people behind Jude. I gave her a nod, and she rolled her eyes. At least I tried.

"Mom gave you money so *we* could have lunch, not just *you*," Jude's little brother Corey pouted.

Corey is one of the smallest sixth graders I had ever seen. He reminded me of Cadence, a lot of whining and a lot of telling.

"I'm buying pizza for both of us, stupid," Jude snapped back. If I'd called Cay any form of the word "stupid," she'd tell Mom. Cadence would tell on me via text, email, or carrier pigeon. She would send a telegram to be sure I was punished. Siblings are the worst.

I must have been grinning because Jude punched me in the arm. "What are you smiling about? I wish Cadence were here to annoy you." I winced as I rubbed the spot he hit.

Cadence and I had a little over five years between us. Thankfully, we'd never have to go to the same school at the same time. I could already see her telling all my business to everyone at school, then going home and telling Mom and Dad everything else.

I ordered a pepperoni pizza and bottled water and waited for Jude. I didn't want water. I just tried really hard not to drink soda. Every time I thought about buying one, I heard my dad's voice – "Athletes don't drink soda. No electrolytes and empty calories." I don't care about electrolytes or calories, but I try to listen to my dad's advice. He doesn't think I listen, but I do... sometimes. It just doesn't seem like it because I mess up a lot. What can I say? I'm human, but I'm trying.

I had no intentions of telling him I had pizza for lunch, though. I won't let him ruin pizza for me, nope. There has to be a line somewhere, I drew it at pizza.

We walked to the benches where most of the team was sitting, and immediately, I could tell something was up.

"*Baby*," I hear from somewhere in the caf, followed by faint laughter.

Oh, no.

"Baby! Baby! BABY," chant about 20 kids, including the entire basketball team.

By the time I turned to the front of the cafeteria, nearly all the 7th graders were in an uproar, laughing and looking at their phones.

Much to my dismay, I had overlooked a vital social media avenue. Everyone was clamoring to get a peek of the video that had run rampant like a virus. How could I have forgotten to check the Gram? I hung my head in defeat. LMS struck again.

I was embarrassed, but I was more disappointed in myself for letting my guard down. I gave the school too much credit, and it took full advantage. Before I could begin my defensive soliloquy, I noticed the mood was surprisingly light. No one was pointing or chastising. No "oohs" or "ahhs." What was going on?

"She can call me baby anytime," someone yelled.

Excuse me? I must have misheard.

"Are your mom and dad still together?"

Another snide remark. I was fuming by this point.

As it turned out, half the boys at school were crushing on my mom. To be honest, that was way worse than teasing, and I wanted to rake every one of them over the coals. I'd rather everyone make fun of me than ask how old my mom was or if my dad was at home. I decided this could very well be the day that I get suspended.

"I'll be your stepdad, Hunt," joked an 8th grader.

I dropped my pizza and squared up, ready to fight. Out of nowhere, Brooke appeared. She picked up my pizza, grabbed my hand, and led me outside the cafeteria—my real-life guardian angel.

"He's not worth it. Your mom is pretty, and you know that. It's better than them calling her ugly," she coached.

"I can't let him disrespect her like that," I replied angrily and adoringly, however that was possible.

I heard distant yelling in the cafeteria. It sounded like girls had started arguing. Normally, I would want to be nosy, but I was so upset I could barely focus on Brooke's words.

"Don't be stupid. You're already in trouble for ignoring Ms. Alex. You think getting into a fight in her honor will make things better? You're trippin' trippin'."

She made an excellent point. I calmed down a little.

"I'll go back in there and tell everyone you wanted to beat him down, but I talked you off the ledge. You won't lose clout. I got you."

"Thank you, B. I really apprecia—"

She was already gone. I sat on a nearby rail and tried to eat my pizza, but I couldn't stop thinking of how thoughtful Brooke had been. She certainly wasn't a mean girl, but she did ruin my lunch again because I couldn't eat. I could only think of her.

***

By the end of the day, things had blown over. Max, the eighth grader, who I almost punched in the face, apologized after school.

"My bad, man," he smiled uneasily. "Honestly, I was just trying to be funny. I'd lose it if someone said something like that about my mom. I know I was wrong."

I just nodded and sauntered off. I was over it, but I wasn't ready to forgive him. A lesson my parents had all but etched into my brain came to mind – our actions have consequences. I'm going to make him feel bad all year. He's going to learn that lesson the hard way.

With an hour between school and practice, I decided to head to the library and get some work done. Normally, I would walk to the store or Burger King around the corner with my teammates, but I wasn't in the mood to run into any of the clowns from school if they still wanted to joke around. I was safe from them in the library – no one ever went to the library.

I walked in with my head down. I didn't want any extra attention. I sat at a lone desk in the corner. It was old and shaky with names and hearts carved into the wood, but it was in a private area. As I pulled my math notebook from my backpack, I noticed Jenn sitting quietly on the bean bags. She was fully engulfed in whatever she was reading. I thought about saying hi. Then, I remembered her reaction from lunch and decided to leave her alone. I didn't need anyone else against me today. I was determined to finish this day better than it had started. My parents always said that the end of a matter was better than its beginning. Today, I'd be pushing that theory to the limit.

I knew that I'd have to have all of my homework done before I got home if I was to escape the full extent of my mom's wrath, so I tackled math first. I only had an hour, so I had to focus.

Twenty-five minutes later, I had finished all but one math problem, and I was feeling confident. I looked up to find that Jenn had already left. I was alone and relieved. Music always helped me through my work, so I grabbed my phone, pressed shuffle, and sang along with one of my favorite songs.

"I had a dream, and I got everything I wanted. Not what you'd think, and if I'm being hone-"

"You got numbers three and four wrong," a low voice interrupted. I nearly jumped out of my skin.

"What?" I asked through a cloud of horror and self-consciousness.

"Number three. The answer is seven over three plus i," Jenn responded matter-of-factly.

Mortified, I asked, "How long have you been standing there?"

"Long enough to know three things. One, you suck at math. Two, you like emo music, and three, you can't sing. Like, at all," she laughed.

"I'm glad you find pleasure in my stupidity. And I wasn't really trying to sing. I was just playing around," I snapped. "I hit those high notes, though," I added jokingly.

"Sure. Anyway, I just finished our math homework if you want help," she offered.

I had 30 minutes left and I thought I was done with math. I still had a little coding to do, plus vocab for Spanish. I couldn't spend any more time on math, but I knew I needed help.

"I still have STEM and some work for Ms. Perez before practice. Can I maybe FaceTime you later for help?" I begged.

"I can't talk to boys on the phone."

Was she serious? I thought my parents were strict.

"Can we meet tomorrow before school? I really need to understand this stuff if I'm going to stay out of trouble with my parents and eligible for the team."

I was desperate.

I could tell she felt sorry for me. Mission accomplished.

"Okay, I guess. I'll meet you by the front office at 7:30. Don't be late," she reluctantly agreed.

Two angels in one day. I should be so lucky!

Chapter Five

Practice was more arduous than usual. I couldn't focus, and Coach's screaming didn't make it any easier. I didn't feel like going through the drills. I was winded, and my mind continued to wander. It must have shown because Coach was on my head.

"Stevens! Why are you walking?"

"Stevens! Hands off your knees."

"Stop talking back!"

By the time we were done with five-on-five, I had looked forward to the tongue-lashing I was going to receive from my mom. Anything was better than the laps and push-ups Coach used as punishment.

The walk home was slow. Not only was I sore, but I also kept going over the way Brooke stood up for me.

The way her curls framed her face made her look like an angel, a mean little angel. It had to be true; she liked me. So, what's next? What do you do when a girl likes you?

In movies, guys buy girls flowers and ask them out. I had seen promposals and stuff like that trending on the Gram. I didn't want to do any of that, though. It seemed like it was too much. I wanted to be more subtle like it didn't matter much. I wished I had an older brother to ask this stuff. My cousin goes to Shadow Ridge. I thought about calling him, but he's a complete nerd. No way he's ever talked to a girl, let alone asked one out.

Then it dawned on me... Brian! He's like the big brother I never had, and he's definitely had plenty of girlfriends. He'll know what to do. I walked faster, with purpose. I needed to get home quietly and track Brian down before my mom took my phone because she was definitely taking it away – it was her go-to punishment.

I decided to go through the backdoor in the kitchen, which led directly to the stairs. With any luck, I'd avoid Mom.

"Hey, Hunt. How was your day?" Mom asked in her normal chipper tone.

What was this trickery?

"Oh, h-hi, Mom. It was fine. I went to the library before practice and got all my homework done," I responded, praying she'd miraculously forgotten about this morning.

Volunteering information about schoolwork was risky since it could jog her solid memory, but I needed her to know I was responsible. Bad kids aren't responsible. Thus, I must be a good kid. It was worth a try.

"That's good. Your father wants to speak with you."

Wait, what? My *father*? I didn't think this warranted a talk with my father. I'm a pretty well-behaved kid. I listen most of the time. In our house, we discuss every little thing. If you're disciplined, you know why, and as long as we're respectful, we're allowed to "argue" our points.

My mom and I usually handle behavioral issues among ourselves. Pops is brought in to reiterate and enforce. So, I was shocked that my mom brought my dad into this. She didn't even call him when my fifth-grade teacher called home after I blurted out, "Deez ----" in class. In my defense, she left herself wide open. I saw the opportunity, and I took advantage. Naturally, my mom chewed me out, and *afterward,* we talked it out with my dad. So, why did she call in the big dog now? This was chump change.

I swallowed hard.

"Daddy?" I asked.

He was always "Daddy" when I was in trouble. Otherwise, I called him Pops.

"Yes, your father. You know, the 6'6" buff guy that lives in my bedroom? Him," she responded sarcastically.

I rolled my eyes. She was being irrational. My dad has the irritating tendency of making mountains out of anthills. Every conversation turns into a life lesson structured around the same three themes:

1. God is love. People should always be able to see God in me.

2. My attitude and effort are all that I can control, so I should put my all into everything I do.

3. I represent God and my parents every time I leave the house – represent them well.

There was no telling how long this would take, and I wanted to call Brian before entering the lion's den.

"Can I take a shower first? I'm stinky from practice." I knew bringing hygiene into the conversation would pique her interest.

"You can do whatever you want. He left early this morning. His platoon is on Shift B," she replied.

My father was a firefighter. His station worked in 48/96 shifts, so he'd be at the station for two days straight then home for four days. Mom was always stressed while he was on, so I tried to be as helpful as possible when he was away. I wished I had known this morning.

"I'm sorry, Mom. I didn't know."

I didn't know what else to say. I felt pretty bad.

She didn't respond. No yelling, no sarcasm. Nothing.

I walked past Cadence, sitting at the table doing homework.

"Hi, Ugly," she quipped.

I ignored her. She was too young to feel the tension in the room, but I was not going to add to it in any way. I walked past her, up the stairs, and directly into my bedroom. Do not pass go; do not collect $200. Callie followed as I closed the door, which I did not plan to open until everyone was asleep.

I flopped onto the welcoming fold of my plush comforter, and a stack of folded clothes fell off the edge of the bed. Mom did most of my laundry, but I had to wash my gym clothes and basketball uniforms. She refused to put folded laundry into my drawers – that was where she drew the line. So, she always left clean, folded clothes on the bed—another example of her Sour Patch personality.

I truly hated disappointing her.

I stared at the ceiling, going over her visit to the school. Was it that big of a deal? I thought maybe it was a bit disrespectful, a tiny bit. I knew she'd be upset, but I didn't imagine she'd be this angry.

There was a soft knock at the door.

"What, Cadence?" I asked impatiently. I wasn't in the mood for her games.

"Can I come in?" she asked. Her little voice sounded so innocent and sweet. How could that tiny voice belong to the little girl who pantsed me at Subway last Thursday?

I didn't want to be bothered. "What do you want?"

"To come in," she snapped. There we go. That's my sister.

"Come in."

"Are you okay?" She seemed genuinely concerned. Did Mom tell her what happened? This thing is really blowing up in my face.

I searched her face for any hint of mockery, to no avail. "I'm good," I replied cautiously. "Are you?"

"I'm okay. Who were you just talking to?" she asked earnestly.

I had developed the habit of thinking aloud. Apparently, I was pondering the day in murmurs.

"I was talking to myself, thinking out loud," I explained.

"Oh. Mommy said you sometimes talked to Granma, so I thought you were sad like her. I'm happy you're not as sad as Mommy. She didn't even make me a snack after school."

Oh, my goodness! This is ridiculous. I merely ignored her. It's not the end of the world. Why was she so dramatic?

"Why is Mommy sad, Cay?" I inquired. Cadence talked a lot, she could barely hold water, so I knew I'd be able to pry it out of her.

"She said Granma Lou died a year ago today, and she misses her a lot."

My heart sank. I sat in a stupor for at least five minutes.

Realizing she no longer had my attention, Cadence walked away. Callie climbed onto the bed and into my lap, bringing me back to reality.

How could I be so dumb? I looked into Callie's furry face. Her eyes, which appeared to be different colors, looked pained as well. Was I the only one oblivious to this anniversary? Was I so wrapped up in girls, school, and basketball that I ignored the things that actually mattered? I was so confused. How was I supposed to know that today was the day? I don't think about the day she passed away very much. It was the saddest day of my life. My parents wouldn't let me see her. They said they didn't want me to remember her sickly. I was really upset with them. I cried into my pillow until I fell asleep. That's all I remember.

The sound of my own voice startled me. I had been thinking aloud again. Mom says that's when I'm talking to Granma, but I felt too ashamed to talk to her. Would she be upset I forgot the day she left us? I forgot her birthday one year, and I was sad because I thought I disappointed her. She grabbed me, looked directly into my eyes, and said, "Life is not the remembering of dates, but the celebrations in between those dates. Last week, you came and had dinner with me. It wasn't my birthday, but you thought about me. That means more to me than an empty phone call today. You had a game. That is your life. You had homework. That is your life. You love me, and I know that because you show me every day, not just on holidays and birthdays. Your heart is so big and so pure. I don't ever want you to think that Granma holds you living your life against you. I've lived my life. I've celebrated lots of birthdays, and now it brings me joy to see you live a full life. So, play hard, work hard, love hard; those are the things that make me happy. Those are the things that make me proud."

I felt better knowing Granma wouldn't be upset with me, but I knew Mom was hurting. I knew she missed her mom. I needed to be there for her.

I ran down the carpeted stairs to find my mom in the kitchen, *not* cooking. She was just standing there. I tapped her shoulder and hugged her. I was about two inches taller than her, and when she hugged me back, I felt the tears from her eyes on my cheek. I cried with her.

Chapter Six

I didn't stay up late. As hard as I fought for an extended bedtime, you'd think I would party all night. Not the case. It was a hard, emotionally draining night.

I felt as heavy as an ogre as I dragged myself out of bed the next morning. I sniffed my armpit and involuntarily shuddered. Like an onion, I was beyond musty. I didn't shower the night before. Instead, I sat in the kitchen with my mom for almost two hours. We talked, she cried, and she yelled. She was frustrated. She was sad. She said she sometimes felt alone. I felt bad for her.

"I want to fix it, Mom. How can I help?" I genuinely implored.

"It's not your problem; it's mine," she replied unsurely. "It isn't even a problem. It's just something I have to deal with – and I'm dealing with it," she added with more confidence.

I pulled back the shower curtain and turned on the water. I didn't feel like fighting with Cadence over bathroom time, so I tried to hurry up. I ran from the bathroom to my room to grab my underwear and towel. On the way back, I tripped over the hallway rug and fell flat on my face.

Mom yelled from upstairs, "Are you okay? What happened?"

"I'm good. I fell, trying to beat Cadence to the bathroom," I screamed as I got up from the floor.

"Trying to beat Cadence? Cadence isn't even here. Are you sure you're okay?"

I walked to Cadence's room for confirmation. No way she was already up and out, it's too early. But sure enough, her bed was neatly made, and her room was spick and span. She's such a goody-two-shoes.

"Where is she?" I asked, somewhat dazed.

"At school."

What? Was I in the twilight zone? It was like 6 am. Even if she had early tests, sending her to school this early would be cruel and unusual. As I limped down the stairs, a little sore from my fall, I noticed how bright it was outside, more than the usual 6 am morning glow.

"Why would she be at school so early? What time is it anyway?" I asked, feeling like I was still in a dream.

"Hunter, it's almost 10:30 in the morning. You overslept, and I didn't want to bother you. You needed a morning for yourself," Mom replied.

It was as if the clouds had separated and a light shone down on her from Heaven as she uttered some of the most beautiful words I had ever heard, quickly followed by my least favorite.

"But you're up now, so go get ready for school."

I rolled my eyes and trudged back up the stairs. I thought I had the day off. That would have been awesome. No math to worry about.

Oh, no! Math! I was supposed to meet Jenn!

I hurriedly showered, brushed my teeth, and got dressed. Mom had made me a bacon and egg sandwich that I ate in the car on the way to school. I was hoping to catch the tail-end of math so that I could apologize to

Jenn. She had been so nice, and I had completely forgotten about her. We had a big test coming up, and I needed her help, so I hoped she would forgive me.

Math was my second class of the day, and class ended at 11:09. I walked onto campus at 10:58 and ran into the office with my mom trailing behind me.

"Bye, Mom," she teased.

After our conversation last night, I made myself a vow to show her a little more love, to let her know that she was appreciated.

"Thanks, Mom. Bye! Have a good day."

I raced to class as she checked me in. I walked into algebra as Mr. Lawson was assigning homework. As soon as I stepped my foot over the threshold, I felt Jenn staring a hole into my skull. This wouldn't be fun.

"Glad you can join us, Mr. Stevens," Mr. Lawson sang.

"Did you miss me, Mr. Lawson?" I asked sarcastically.

He turned and smiled, "We all missed you so much that we completed two lessons today that you'll have to catch up to finish."

"Everyone's a comedian," I mumbled under my breath as I hung my head.

I sloppily jotted down the assignments. As everyone started to pack up, I turned to Jenn.

"Jenn, I'm so sorry," I pleaded.

"Do not talk to me. Ever," she replied coldly.

"Please. Listen. I – I didn't mean to," I tried to reply.

"I never should have trusted you. I shouldn't have agreed to meet you. I blame myself, not you, but I won't fall for it again. So, no, I won't listen. Goodbye, Hunter."

She stood up and walked away without looking back. Wow.

I stood there shook.

"Hunter, I know you just joined us, but class is over. Unless you want to stay for the next class, I'd like you to go, please," Mr. Lawson joked.

I stepped into the hall and scanned the crowd for Jenn. I saw Leslie, Jordan, April, Maya, Jessica, India, Brooke (oh, hey, Brooke), Meaghan, and Kristina. I saw every seventh-grade girl at LSM, but not Jenn. I walked through the hall past Brooke without speaking, she trailed me with her eyes full of confusion. I suppose she was used to me acknowledging her presence. I didn't have time to talk to her. I had to find Jenn. Adding two assignments pushed me well past desperate.

Lunch was starting, so I went straight to the cafeteria. I saw her in the pizza line the day before. I figured maybe I'd get lucky and she wanted pizza again today. No such luck. Where did she hang out at lunch? Now that I think about it, before yesterday, I never saw her outside of math.

I saw Matt, a kid in our math class, and I asked if he knew where Jenn hung out. He didn't even know who she was. No bueno. How could I beg for forgiveness if I couldn't even find her?

I spent all of lunch looking for her. I started in the caf, and then I looked on the yard, in the gym, and on the quad... she was nowhere to be found.

Heading to sixth period, I realized I was on my own. Math Club wasn't going to be enough to get me through. I couldn't let the team down, but I really didn't get it. I knew I needed help, and I probably blew my best chance of getting it. I decided to go to Mr. Lawson for help after school. Teachers always say they're here for you and they want you to succeed. Let's see if he meant it.

After school, I decided to peek into the library, a final attempt to find and plead with Jenn.

Another L.

I ran to Mr. Lawson's class, hoping to catch him before he went home. I skidded past the door and fell from running so fast. Today was not a good equilibrium day. Mr. Lawson poked his head out of his classroom.

"Are you okay?"

Flushed faced, I responded, "Yes. I'm fine. Thank you. I was trying to catch you before you left."

"Hunter? Is that you," he questioned. "I thought you'd be more agile, being a student-athlete and all."

"I actually came to talk to you about that," I responded sheepishly.

"Step into my office," he said as he mockingly ushered me into the class.

I pled my case, expressing my desire to play and feigned interest in math. He didn't buy it, but because I always worked hard and behaved well, he agreed to assign me a tutor who I could see in place of Math Club. I had to agree to meet with them a half-hour before school every day and an additional hour twice a week. I excitedly agreed. He would assign the tutor, and our first session would be at 7:30 the next morning.

Mr. Lawson also agreed to change the due date of my make-up work until after the weekend. I was so thankful! I wanted to do flips, but I had to run to practice. If I were late, I'd have to run laps. I was sick of running.

"Before you stumble off," he called to me as I walked away, "I think the tutor is in Ms. Morris's class right now. Hold on."

He peeked his head through the door and yelled.

"Ms. Morris, is your little helper still in there?"

"Yep," Ms. Morris sang.

I stood there, impatiently. Was I supposed to say something? Should I walk toward the class? I looked at Mr. Lawson as if he could hear the questions I was asked in my mind.

He nodded his head toward Ms. Morris's class.

What did that mean?

I looked at her door just as Jenn stepped out.

"Your new tutor."

Perfect!

Chapter Seven

Do you know what's crazy about dreams? In a dream, you can perfectly recall a place you've never been, down to the last detail – the smell of freshly cut grass, a stranger's accent, the sound of the chirping smoke detector (Why is it that no one ever changes the battery on those things? They beep for days!). Dreams are crazy like that, and last night's dream was definitely crazy.

I don't remember falling asleep, but I do remember texting Brian to ask for his advice. It had been an insane week, but I was convinced that Brooke liked me more than ever. So, after "the talk" with my dad (stick a pin in that, I'll definitely get back to it), I really wanted to see what Brian thought. He didn't text me back, which was cool because I had a lot of math to do. Jenn was strict, like a teacher, and I really did not want to let her down again, so I was doing algebra in my dreams... literally.

It was halftime of a playoff game. We were the visiting team, down 163 points. Coach was going over the opening play, but I was at the end of the bench, computing an algebra equation with numbers and symbols floating over my head like a cartoon. The court was freshly polished, and the fumes were giving me a headache. I reached to hold my throbbing head, and I mixed up the numbers.

I could hear my mom screaming from the bleachers, "Defense! D up!"

I usually ignored my mom during games, but it was halftime. There was no one on the court, not even the cheerleaders. I stood up to yell at her, and out of nowhere, my dad appeared, standing directly in front of her, in full turnout gear with his arms crossed angrily. He was wearing a face shield, but I could feel the anger in his eyes, burning a hole through my soul, so I sat down quickly.

When I sat down, I was somewhere else, but I don't know where. While I had never been there before, it smelled familiar, like Gram. I liked it there until a witch stormed in on a broom, flying around like a mosquito. I was so irritated, so annoyed that she would violate such a peaceful place. I tried to swat her down. I was swinging so frantically that I smacked myself dead in the face, hard. Fed up, I tried to wake myself. I closed my eyes and screamed as loud as I could, only to find myself back at the game, dribbling down the court. I looked for the outlet pass, but nothing was there, so I stopped and shot a pull up.

Bucket.

I read the defense and got a quick steal, threw it up to my big man, who I had never seen before in my life, for an easy lay. The crowd booed as the buzzer sounded. We won by four, and I woke up.

What the heck?

Chapter Eight

My dad came home in a bad mood from his shift. I tried to steer clear of him because I didn't know if he was still upset with me. I tiptoed around the house all day long, sneaking to get snacks and to use the bathroom. It didn't help that I couldn't go anywhere until I caught up on my math. Yeah, I was almost done with everything, but being told I couldn't go anywhere made me want to go everywhere. I texted all of my friends to see what they were doing. No one had a life. The only thing any of us ever did was play basketball. Maybe I wasn't as popular as I thought.

Saturday night was the first time my dad spoke to me.

"Hi, Son," he asserted.

"Oh, h-hi, Pop," I stammered. "How was your shift?"

"It was tough, Son. I saw a family lose everything they had," he replied with a sad look in his eyes. "They went out to dinner without a care in the world and came home to ashes. Weeks like this, I question how long I can keep this up."

"You once told me that you are called to help others, that your job was important to you because helping people is important to you. Has that changed?"

"Not at all, Son," he answered with a hint of optimism. "Not at all. Thanks for the reminder."

Proud of myself, I countered, "Any time, Pop. That's what I'm here for."

With my head high, I started for the stairs.

"Hold up," he stopped me in my tracks. "I've been watching you creep around the house, avoiding me. At first, I was cool with it. It was nice to have a little peace and quiet. Then, Cadence started bothering *me,* so I need you to snap out of it. What's going on, anyway?"

What's going on? Clearly, he forgot about our "talk," so I had to maneuver my way out of this one.

"Nothing. I just have a lot of math to catch up on, so I was focused. Besides, I could tell you weren't in the best mood, so I didn't want to bother you. You know, I was looking out for you... trying to be considerate."

He eyed me suspiciously. I may have gone too far.

"Oh, you were looking out for *me*? How considerate of you! Kind of the same way you looked out for your mom earlier this week, huh?"

Ah, there it is. He played me.

"What's going on with you, Hunt? We expected some changes as you got older, but to be so inconsiderate to your mother – that ain't it, Buddy."

I didn't know what to say. He was right. I felt the sting of tears forming in my eyes, and I hated myself for it. I always cried when confronted, and it made me feel like a baby. I tried to stop them from falling, but I felt one warm droplet ease its way down my cheek.

The look on my dad's face changed as he watched the tears roll toward my chin.

"Talk to me, Son," he begged.

"Pop, I didn't mean to ignore Mom. It's just that she was screaming my name and walking around school, calling me 'baby.' It was so embarrassing."

My reply was intense, much more emotional than I had intended.

"You think we care about that?" he laughed. The sound of laughter made me feel a little better. "I'm sure your Mom did that on purpose. She lives to get you back for all the silly little things you're always doing."

I knew it! I always had a feeling she was being intentionally obtuse. She knew the consequences I'd have to face from my unforgiving peers. Oh, this meant war.

I didn't have time to begin to devise a plan of revenge before my short-lived sense of vengeance was snuffed out with my dad's next words.

"I'm talking about your grandmother."

The tears came back. I couldn't stop them, and I didn't try.

I hung my head low. "I- I didn't know, Daddy."

Any time I felt vulnerable, I crawled into a shell of my childhood self. I was five years old again, and my dad became Daddy. I needed him to understand how sorry I was, how bad I felt that I had hurt my mom. I peeked my head out like a reluctant turtle.

"There's no way I would've even asked her to come to the school if I had known. When I got home, Cay told me, and I felt so bad. Really, Dad. I know how much Mom misses Granma Lou. I miss Granma, too. A whole lot. I told her everything. Now, I have no one to talk to about Brooke or Jenn, no one to vent to."

At this point, the tears were streaming. I was talking fast and breathing heavily. Dad held my shoulder and pulled me into his chest.

"I'm sorry, Son. I never considered that you lost your best friend, too."

It wasn't until that very moment that I realized that Granma Lou was my best friend.

"You shouldn't be responsible for your mother's feelings," Dad continued. "I was expecting too much of you. That's on me."

This was unchartered territory. *Dad* was apologizing to *me*.

"It's okay, Pop. I should've known," I admitted.

"No. That's not right. If you had remembered on your own, then that's fine, but to be required to remember is not fair. You are a chi-. My bad. You are a teenager. You get to be young and carefree for as long as you can. Right now, you are somewhere between being a kid and a young adult. Once you cross that threshold, things get real serious, real quick, and you're right at the cusp. I'll give you this instance as long as you realize childish things are coming to an end. I'm sure you're noticing that more and more every day."

He was right. My parents talked a lot about ending generational curses and empowering Cay and me to be better than they were. It never made much sense to me, but as I watched my dad try to understand me and not just yell and punish, I saw that he was trying to be a good father, and he was a good father. Maybe he didn't know it.

I wiped my tears and assured my father. "Thanks, Pop. That means a lot. I want to grow up, though. I want to do better."

"Just be mindful of other people's feelings. Pay attention, not just to what they say but how they act.

That's a big part of growing up, caring about people's feelings."

"Okay, I'll try," I replied. That seemed tough, though. I never know what people are feeling, especially girls.

As if he were reading my mind, Dad asked, "Now, who's Jenn? And what about Brooke?"

I wasn't ready to tell Mom and Dad that I liked Brooke. There would be way too many questions and jokes. I didn't even notice I had mentioned Jenn. Why did I bring her up?

"Jenn is my math tutor. She's strict like a teacher, so it's been hard working with her, but I understand better. I guess that's a plus."

I changed the subject, hoping he wouldn't ask about Brooke again.

"Are you going to be able to make it to my game tomorrow?"

Basketball was always a go-to topic with my dad. He was always willing to talk ball.

"Yessir!" he responded excitedly. "I haven't been to a game in a while. I can't wait to see you out there. Are you ready?"

"What? I'm always ready. I stay ready," I exclaimed enthusiastically.

The truth was I was eager to play in front of my father. I had improved a lot since he'd seen me play last. I knew he'd be impressed by my growth.

"Don't get too cocky now," he teased. "Leave it all on the court. That's all I ever ask. Play hard and play smart. Let your game speak for itself."

"I know, I know. I'm going to get buckets, though."

"I expect nothing less," he said. As we high-fived, he grabbed my arm and pulled me into a hug. "I hope you're never too old to hug your old Pop."

Secretly, I hoped the same.

Chapter Nine

It wasn't a regular Monday. To start, I finished all my Algebra homework with ease. I was beginning to understand it, thanks to Jenn. I was in such a good mood that I woke up early and walked Cadence to school. My beautiful little monster talked my ear off the entire time, something about being a millionaire and making Mom proud. I would smile, nod, and ask an occasional question, so she didn't think I ignored her, but I had no idea what she was talking about, and I didn't really care. All I could think about was how excited Jenn would be when she saw how well I did on all my work. I had Mom check everything to make sure it was perfect.

When I got back home, Mom was waiting to take me to school. Before she checked my work, I told her about my agreement with Mr. Lawson, and it seemed I gave her a new purpose in life because she won't leave me alone about getting my work done and being on time for my sessions. She was in the driveway with the window rolled down, screaming to me from down the street.

"C'mon, Hunter, Baby," she chanted.

It was hard to believe she was using my teenaged angst as entertainment. Wait, no, it wasn't. Mom always told me not to take everything so seriously that there would come a time when life had to be serious, and I'd regret stressing over trivial things. She didn't understand that this was serious, as serious as it gets for a 13-year-old. I took a deep breath and ran to the car.

"Mom, you aren't funny," I huffed. "That was embarrassing. Why are you like this?"

"I'm sorry, but you are my baby. You will always be my baby," she smiled sheepishly.

I was mad, I wanted to stay mad, but I couldn't. I could never stay mad at her. It was annoying.

"I made you honey buns," she added as she shoved two huge cinnamon rolls into my hand. They were still warm, so the icing slid off the wax paper. See, I told you – sour then sweet. Impossible to stay mad.

I took a big bite, and with a mouth full of food, I attempted to speak.

"I haf ta git mah bags an my pone."

Her eyes widened, and she shook her head slightly. "Excuse me?"

I didn't try again. I didn't want the lecture about talking with my mouth full. I jogged away from the car toward the house. I found all my things waiting by the door. Sour then sweet, yet again.

I strolled back to the car, hands and heart full.

Mom played my music in the car and drove directly to the front entrance.

Monday: redefined.

Jenn was standing at the front gate with her arms crossed, tapping her foot. Sheesh! I wasn't even late.

"Good morning, Jenn!" I sang, determined to spread love and good cheer.

"No," was her only verbal response, but she pretty much cut me with her eyes. Man, she was the mean girl.

"Thank you for helping him, Sweetheart," my mom called from the car. "I'll make sure he is on top of his work and doesn't waste your time."

Jenn perked up.

"Good morning, Mrs. Stevens," she said and shot me the evilest look. "It's my absolute pleasure to work with Hunter. Thank you for your help with getting him on time. After he left me here all alone last week, no call or anything, I wasn't sure if he'd show up."

Oh, she's ruthless.

"He what?!" Mom shrieked. "I'm so sorry, Sweetie. I had no idea."

Mom didn't realize that was the morning she let me sleep in, but for some strange reason, I knew she wasn't going to care.

"Hunter, I don't believe you! How incredibly inconsiderate! We will talk about this later. Don't you waste another minute of this precious darling's time. Get inside right now!"

Jenn smiled with complete and utter satisfaction as she grabbed my backpack strap and pulled me inside. I dragged my feet, dumbstruck, as I watched my mom sneer and drive away.

What was happening?

This was slowly turning into the Mondayist of Mondays.

***

School was completely uneventful. Classes were boring, Jenn was not impressed by my newfound mathematical genius (as she put it, "You should've already known this stuff. You want me to reward mediocrity?"), and Brooke ignored me, as usual.

None of that mattered, though. Today was game day, and my focus had already shifted. I wasn't worried about classes, girls, or my parents. I was only interested in getting this dub. Actually, I was thinking about my dad a teeny tiny bit. I was excited he was coming to the game. I had added a few moves to my repertoire, and I knew he wouldn't be expecting them. I couldn't wait to see the look on his face, watching me hit Kobe's signature fadeaway jumper. I'd been watching video for weeks and working on it in the backyard when I had time. I thought I had it down, and I was ready for its debut.

My game day routine was simple – headphones, Travis Scott playlist on shuffle, my ball, and ten minutes of uninterrupted dribbling, between my legs, behind my back, with two balls, with a tennis ball, and crossover, two minutes each. Coach knew my process, and he respected it, one of the only things he respected.

After my drills, I joined the lay-up line, just as they opened the gym to parents and students. My mom was one of the first ones in the gym. I knew this because Cadence ran onto the court as soon as she saw me. I've asked Mom to stop her. She said Cay is my biggest fan, and I should "embrace her support." I've gotten used to it, so I hugged her and quickly shooed her away. She eagerly ran to Mom, who mouthed a quick "thank you."

After warm-ups, Coach went over the game plan one last time. We were two games away from the playoffs. We had already secured a berth, but there was a possibility we'd play this team in the second round, so we had to show them we were ready and they should be worried.

As Coach would say, "Set the tone."

The first half was extremely competitive. I didn't expect to work so hard on defense, but it fueled my offense. I had a good game, nothing too extreme. I was waiting for Dad to arrive so I could really show out. The second half was mine.

As if she were reading my mind, Mom walked over to the bench and whispered to my coach.

My heart started to pound out of my chest. Last year, I had to leave a game after a similar exchange. I still hadn't recovered.

Where was my dad?

My eyes started to water. I jumped up from the bench and ran to my mom.

"What's going on? Where's Dad? Mom, what's up? Mom!"

I hadn't given her a chance to respond. I was completely freaking out.

Mom grabbed my shoulders and looked into my eyes, "Hunter, your father is —"

I blacked out. She was talking, and I saw her mouth moving, but I couldn't hear her. I assumed the worst, and I wasn't ready to deal with any more loss. I was gone. I was with Granma Lou. I felt Cadence grab my hand. My beautiful little monster needed me.

"Hunter, did you hear me?" Mom asked as she wiped a rogue tear from my face.

"Your father is fine. His company was called to San Luis Obispo to help contain a growing fire. It has already burned nearly 3,000 acres."

I'd never been more relieved.

I looked over at Coach Hill, who had a genuine look of concern on his face. I nodded to assure him I was okay.

"Mom, can you record the game on your phone, please? I want to send the video to Pop."

"Of course, Honey. Whatever you want," she agreed and reached for her dated Android.

"You have to get a new phone, Mom," I teased as I ran back to the bench as they were breaking for the second half.

I said a prayer for my dad and the other firemen before I torched Hamilton Intermediate.

We lost on a lucky buzzer-beater, despite my 23-point contribution. I was crushed. Even though I had an amazing game, the win would've been better. Coach reminded us that losing was a part of the game and that learning from our losses is just as important as winning. I didn't agree, but I listened.

Mom was talking to a group of parents near the car. She gave me a hug that lasted a little too long and asked if I wanted In-N-Out for dinner.

It was a good Monday, after all. I knew it would be.

Chapter Ten

Dad was in California for four days. We talked every day while he was gone. He explained where he was and how the fire was burning. Santa Ana winds were fighting against him and the other smokejumpers. I wasn't worried about him, though, because I knew he was covered. I was proud. I wanted him to be proud of me, so I edited all the videos that my mom recorded during my game and sent them to him. I had to change the background music because Mom was screaming throughout the whole thing.

"Defense... That's a foul, ref... Hold your follow-through," and my all-time favorite free throw-ism, "Take your time, Baby! You've got this!"

I think she thinks that she's a sideline coach. I also think she's horribly annoying.

Two minutes after I sent the video, my phone rang. "Pop" appeared on the screen with my favorite picture of my father. Imagine a 30-something-year-old man being thrown into the sky on water skis. Now imagine that man doing splits in the air. Ladies and gentlemen, Pop. That photo was a great representation of who he was as a person – bold, fearless, uncoordinated, and agile.

"I didn't know you had Kobe's jumper in your bag!" Dad exclaimed. "That made my day! It looks like you had a great game, playing the right way. I'm proud of you. I'm sorry I couldn't make it, though. Another missed game. I hate disappointing you, Son."

"You are where you're supposed to be. I'm not disappointed," I shared earnestly.

"Thank you for understanding, but it's hard to forgive myself. You'll understand when you have kids."

Welp, that settled it. I'll never understand because I'm most definitely not having kids. Too much work, too much stress. Cadence drives me crazy, and she's just my sister. What if I had a kid like her? I'd run away from home.

I started rummaging through the text messages on my phone. "I don't know, Pop. It's pretty easy to forgive me."

He smiled. I could hear it.

"Boy, you're something else," he laughed. "Let me speak to your mother. I love you, and I'm proud of you. You're the man of the house while I'm gone. Hold it down."

I pressed mute and screamed for Mom.

"Mother! Your husband would like to speak with you."

"Stop yelling in the house," she screamed.

Oh, the irony.

I looked in the mirror as if I were in a movie and shrugged. If this were, indeed, a movie, this scene would end with a clip of my video with cinematic music playing in the background, except this wasn't a movie, and the soundtrack to my highlights was played by the great poet, Travis Scott.

Mom walked into the room while I was staring in the mirror, deep in thought.

"Studying your face?" she quizzed. "I see a few pimples brewing. You haven't been washing your face with the cleanser I bought you."

How did she have the ability to turn everything into a "Mom moment" – you know, when a simple question turns into an hour-long lecture or an awkward encounter? Ladies and gentlemen, Mom.

"I've been using the cleanser, Mom," I responded honestly.

"Well, it certainly doesn't look like it," she snapped.

I wanted to tell her that she didn't know everything, that there were plenty of things she couldn't tell simply by looking at them, but I knew for a fact that would be a serious tongue lashing, so I refrained.

"Maybe I need to use it more often," I said with a smile. "I'll start using it at night, too."

She was very pleased with my response. She kissed my forehead as she took the phone from my hand. I really knew how to work a room. Why couldn't I do that with Brooke or Jenn? Why did Jenn keep creeping into my thoughts?

"Hey, Babe," she crooned into the phone, "I'll call you from my phone. Hello? Hel-lo?" she screamed (again) into the phone.

"I muted it, Mom."

"Oh," she said as she looked at the screen and lightly tapped the illuminated microphone and laughed. "Why do you love this picture of your dad so much? Oh, Brian just texted you."

Brian! I'd been waiting to hear from him for what seemed like a week. I grabbed the phone from her hands and sat on the edge of my bed.

"I'llcallyoufrommyphone," Mom said quickly as the distance between her and the phone increased.

I hung up the call and shooed her out of the room. I needed privacy.

How should I go about this? Do I bring it up casually or come right out and ask? My text to him was pretty vague.

Hey, Brian, I kinda need your help. Text me when you can. No rush or anything. It really isn't a big deal. K, ttyl.

I didn't want to seem desperate. I decided not to mention Brooke because that would probably make it weird. Brian probably looked at her like a little sister. I didn't want to upset him with the idea. Then it dawned on me – Dom. I'd have to deal with his nonsense, questions, jokes, and probably physical assault, but she was worth it. Brooke was worth dealing with a hundred Doms. Besides, once they see how happy we are together, Dom and Brian will be happy for us.

Our conversation started off rocky, so I decided to get right to it.

Brian: *Who is this?*

Me: *It's Hunter. Sorry, I thought you had my #.*

Brian: *Oh, hey, Hunt. I got a new phone. No numbers. What's up?*

Me: *Um, I kinda need some advice.*

Brian: *Ok…*

Me: *It's about a girl.*

Brian: *Oh. I don't know if I'm the best guy to ask. You should text Dom.*

Me: *No. I don't want Dom in my business. Besides, he's a jerk, and I really like this girl.*

Brian: *I guess you're right. What do you need to know?*

Me: *I want to ask this girl out. I'm sure she likes me, but I get so nervous around her. What should I say? Should I text her, call her, talk to her at school? I'm lost.*

Brian: *You want to go out like on a date or you want her to be your gf?*

Me: *I guess a date first, but I've never been on a date either. I don't even know if my parents would let me go.*

Brian: *So...*

Me: *Let me call my dad. I'll hit you back.*

Talking to my dad wouldn't be so bad. I just know he'll ask questions, and I'm positive he'll tell my mom. I know she already suspected something. Hopefully, she'd be cool about this.

I called my dad. No answer. I stuck my head out of my door and yelled down the stairs, "Mom, are you still on the phone with Pop?"

"Yes, he said he'll call you when we hang up," she replied.

Great, they'll be on the phone all night. I picked up the phone to text my dad, only to find one last text from Brian.

Write her a letter.

Don't be corny and don't pour your heart out.

Tell her you like her and you want to take her to the movies.

Don't give her a chance to say no. Tell her when and where.
Shoot your shot.

"Shoot your shot." I was good at that.

Chapter Eleven

My grades were really coming together. My low C had fallen to a high D between progress reports, but Mom had been busy with other things and hadn't checked the parent portal. Thankfully, I pulled it up to a high C in a week, saving myself from a barrage of lectures and punishments. Mr. Lawson was impressed. I tried to take credit, but he knew it was Jenn. I knew it was Jenn, too, but she was such a little tyrant that she made it hard to give her props. I was on time for all our scheduled meetings, and she was still mean, like an angry little bumblebee, buzzing around and stinging me without cause.

I was proud that my next progress report would boast a hard-earned 3.0 grade point average. Mom would be pleased, and Dad would definitely find a way to reward my efforts. Things were looking up, and when my grades were good, everything else fell into place. I tried to explain to my parentals how my quality of life was directly linked to my grades, but they didn't listen.

Hear me out – When I struggled in a class, I stressed because both basketball and my PlayStation privileges were threatened, those being my two absolute favorite things in the world. Protecting them became a priority, and I would start to feel the weight of the world on my shoulders. Talk about stressful, and when I'm stressed, my attitude is less than pleasant. Mom has gone as far as to call me obnoxious. That is clearly her flawed perception because I am, without a doubt, a beacon of joy at all times. However, I have been known to kick, fight, and scream when I'm in what Mom calls a "mood." Even Cadence steers clear when I'm out of sorts.

This "mood" also tends to get me in trouble at school. Smart remarks and snapping at teachers are kind of frowned upon, but they generally get the brunt of my wrath because it is, after all, ultimately their fault. Teachers are rarely willing to take the blame for their part in these exchanges, which usually end in a nicely worded email to my parents or, in severe cases, a dreaded phone call home. Calls home upset my parents and lead to the inevitably feared loss of privileges. It's a vicious cycle, very ugly, very unnecessary, and very rarely my fault.

Fortunately, this wasn't my current predicament. Actually, I was expecting the exact opposite. My good grades should encourage my parents to be extra generous, which, in turn, would improve my disposition, a beautiful exchange that encouraged me to work harder at school and home. My chores were always done without having to be told. Well, almost always – the toilet was beyond a chore, more like a punishment that my mom wielded over me. I waited for her to threaten me before I ever cleaned that thing. I get the heebie geebies just thinking about it.

Between my schoolwork, homework, and basketball, I didn't have time for anything else, but I was on a roll.

Dad was finally home and had caught a few games. I had been balling. His face beamed with pride as he watched me play. After games, he'd always say, "I love watching you play, but basketball was my dream. You know it doesn't have to be yours."

Dad's hoop dreams turned into nightmares when he was a kid. He had a seizure on the court when he was my age, and his parents wouldn't let him play anymore. That's why Mom came to all my games and watched me like a hawk. They were never able to tell him the cause of the seizures, and they magically stopped when he was in high school.

He says he was good, but I know I'm better.

I was super content with life in my little bubble. School, basketball, home, repeat. I would write Brooke's letter at some point, I was building up confidence. In the meanwhile, I enjoyed being her friend. Initially, I was on a recon mission – find out as much as I could and go in for the kill. It was so much easier to talk to her without the pressure of saying the right or wrong thing. I could be dumb with her. She laughed at all my jokes, we talked on the phone all the time, and she came to my games. It was as if being myself was enough. Nah, no way.

Things were good, though. I had no intention of messing them up.

***

Being the good guy was working in my favor. Until now, my parents were very wary of video blogs. I asked for a channel for two years, and the answer was always a resounding no. I thought about going behind their backs and starting a channel without their permission, but something told me that would be a bad idea. As if it were confirmation from above, my friend, Evan, was busted with a secret Instagram account the next day. He got in big trouble. I didn't want that for my life, so I decided to keep things on the up and up.

Frustrated with rejection, I stopped asking for a channel months ago but continued to watch my favorite streamer almost every day. I was only allowed to play video games on the weekends, so watching him play was the next best thing. One day, Mom heard me listening and angrily stormed into my room.

"Are you really playing that game on a school night?" she accused.

"No," I asserted. "I'm watching the Twitcher stream."

"Who is Twitcher Stream," she asked mindlessly.

"Twitcher is a stream*er*," I laughed and showed her my Chromebook screen.

"Oh. Is that on 'the Tube'?" she asked.

"Yep. Don't worry. He doesn't curse or play any killing games."

She looked at me and smiled, "I trust you, Son. You know the rules, and I trust you to obey them."

Then, there was a shockingly pleasant follow-up, "Do you still want a video page of your own?"

"Uh, yeah, I still want a channel!" I almost yelled.

"Your dad and I discussed it, and we think maybe…" she paused and looked at her nails, leaving me in the longest state of limbo.

"MOM!"

"We think you're ready to have a channel," she said, unsure of the proper terminology.

I jumped up and hugged her.

She said I had shown such growth over the last few weeks, and they would let me try the channel on a trial basis. The catch was that the page had to be private until they were comfortable with "exposing me to the world."

I was okay with that. It made our channel exclusive, and an invite would be sought after!

Our first few videos were basic — Fortnite streams and simple vlogs. We didn't know who to send invites to, so we started with the basketball team. We were the only players on the team with a channel, so they loved it. They all wanted to be in our videos. Before we knew it, most of the eighth-grade boys and a few from other middle schools were on our invite list.

We suddenly had more popularity than we were prepared to deal with, and that wasn't a good thing.

Chapter Twelve

We decided to name our channel "Bucket Bros," or "BB," as I affectionately coined it. Jude was our Fortnite expert, and I covered basketball. Finding time to record became an immediate problem. Jude and I had pretty much the same school and basketball schedule, but math tutoring and homework ate a huge chunk of our streaming time. Another stipulation to keep BB alive was that my schoolwork could never suffer. My grades had to stay the same or better, or I was out. What a tall order!

I tried to butter up my parents and throw a postdated excuse on the table.

"I really appreciate your confidence in me and your reward for my hard work. I promise to keep it up. I'd hate to let you down."

"We know you can keep it all up," Mom remarked as she folded laundry. "Time management and prioritizing will be very important. This is an opportunity for you to learn and grow. Being able to manage your academic, athletic, and social calendars will be a useful tool as you grow older."

She turned everything into a "learning moment."

"I'm going to step up. You'll see," I retorted. "But," I added, "I wanted to let you know ahead of time that exams next quarter will be hard. My teachers have already said that not many As will be handed out.

I peered at her from the corner of my eye, wondering if she took the bait.

"Good thing you've been working so hard," my dad chimed in. "You'll be one of the few!"

His sarcasm was thick. He wasn't going for it, but there was always hope with Mom. You could never discount her empathy.

I planned on working hard, regardless. I simply needed them to know what I was up against and have a safeguard in place in case things went awry. BB was quickly overtaking basketball and video games in my hierarchy of entertainment. I really enjoyed it.

"You've got this, Son," Mom cheered.

She was positive, and I was already getting anxious. I just had to stay focused; it couldn't be that hard.

We had already posted three videos, one for each of our specialties, and a vlog that we filmed at school during lunch, after school, and basketball practice. The vlog was the most fun because our teammates were able to hop on camera. There were always lots of jokes and laughs. Sometimes, the jokes were at the expense of others, but it was never anything too bad – just playful banter – you know, good fun.

Coach allowed us to film the beginning of practice, our stretches, and warm-ups. Then, the camera had to go off. Playoffs were scheduled to start the next week, and we needed to "hunker down" and commit.

Practices were tough, too—lots of up and down, new plays, and contact. Coach said we needed to toughen up, but I was more like beat up. I went home sore for the first few days and passed out as soon as I hit my bed. Neither Jude nor I gave BB a second thought. We went a week without a video, and for the entire week, I received texts and messages - guys from my school — begging for another episode. They even had topic suggestions:

1. Best and worst Lawrence SA teachers
2. Top five NBA players
3. Top ten Fortnite skins
4. Ranking Lawrence SA girls.

I immediately decided against numbers one and four. I knew better. They were bound to get us in trouble, and I worked diligently to stay off the proverbial naughty list.

I was really excited about compiling my top five list. I decided to throw in a player most would think unworthy of top-five status to stir up a little controversy. I spent my small window of free time between school and practice preparing for the video. I researched stats, salaries, and all-star ballots. I went all out. I was so deep in thought that I didn't notice Brooke standing over my shoulder.

"What class is this for?" she questioned skeptically.

"This isn't for school," I answered proudly. I was becoming oddly cocky and protective over our project. It was my baby. "This is for Bucket Bros., my video channel."

"Oh," she replied unenthusiastically. "Stupid boy stuff."

"Whatever," I sneered as I pushed her away. "Why are you still here? School has been over for 30 minutes."

As the question came out of my mouth, three things happened simultaneously: 1. I remembered I was missing a session with Jenn – she was going to kill me. 2. The ever-looming thought of Brooke's letter gave me pause. 3. I saw Jenn glaring a hole through my soul from what seemed like a mile away.

"Brian said he'd walk me home today, so I'm just waiting for him…" she yammered, but I had already drowned her out, something my mom said Dad does all the time. I was trained on Jenn's distant face. Initially, it seemed she wore an expression of anger that transformed into disappointment. I even thought I caught a hint of sadness, but she was so far away, I couldn't tell. I stood up to go to her, but she walked away. I picked up my phone to text her and saw that I was about to be late for practice. I threw my Chromebook into my backpack and ran as fast as I could to the gym.

I ran past the cafeteria and main office buildings. Mrs. L was standing outside with a crying sixth grader — surely their mom or dad was late picking them up. She would sit there with them until they showed up. She's so sweet.

"No running on campus, Mr. Stevens," she called. "Be careful. If you move too fast, you'll pass your future."

I stopped altogether. What in the world did that mean? I turned around and walked quickly toward her.

"I'm sorry, Mrs. L," I apologized. "I don't want to be late for practice. Is everything okay here?"

"Oh, yes. Matthew is waiting for his dad. We're going to sit here together until he makes it from work. Aren't we, Matt?"

Matt didn't even look at her. His eyes were bloodshot red. I knew he was embarrassed.

"Last year, I missed my bus, and Mrs. Lattimore waited an hour with me after school," I recalled. "You're in good hands, Matt. Do you want to wait in the gym while we practice?"

He looked at me with woeful eyes, softening into a smile.

"C'mon. You can call your dad from my phone and let him know where you're waiting. I got him, Mrs. L," I assured her. "By the way, what did you mean about passing my future?"

Her perplexed look confused me.

"I didn't say anything about your future, Boy," she looked at me as if I was crazy. She's getting up there. She must've already forgotten.

Older people are always forgetting things or telling the same story over and over.

"When I was running, you told me to slow down, or I'll pass my future," I tried to jog her memory.

Her expression never changed. "I said no such thing. Are you okay?"

Without saying a word, Matt shook his head, seemingly in agreement with her.

Was I tripping?

I heard her loud and clear, almost as if she were in my head. Then, it dawned on me – it had been in my head. It was Granma Lou's voice, clear as day.

Chapter Thirteen

Playoffs were upon us, and my focus simply wasn't, well, focused. I had too many outside distractions vying for my attention. I owed it to my team to concentrate, chew up our opponents, and spit them out. However, I was merely storing them in my cheeks like a chipmunk before relaxing my jaw and allowing them to escape.

Luckily, we won our first game by the hair of our chins, though none of us had any chin hair. After the game, Coach let me have it. Actually, he let all of us have it, but I took it personally because I knew I could have done more.

"Whether a starter or a role player, I can accept any player having a bad game, but what I cannot and will not tolerate is lackadaisical running up and down the court. If you want to play, *play*. If you want to play around, go to a park."

Coach was right.

My dad mirrored his emotions. His delivery was a bit softer, but the message was the same.

"Son, you didn't look like you wanted to be out there. No one is forcing you to play, but if you're going to go out there, you have to leave it all on the court. You never know who's watching."

Who was watching was my exact problem.

Brooke continued to come to all the games, which I was used to at this point. She didn't come to actually watch the game, just gossip and flip her hair around. It was Jenn who started showing up to games that rattled me. She hadn't talked to me in a week and wouldn't listen anytime I tried to explain to her why I wasn't at our tutoring session. I was convinced she only showed up to games to get under my skin, and I was upset it worked. I couldn't get her out of my head, and it bothered me… a lot. Why did it even matter? She made it completely obvious that she wanted nothing to do with me.

I had violated the terms of our agreement, so Mr. Lawson left it up to her whether she wanted to continue tutoring me – she chose not to continue. So, if she didn't want to tutor me, why this sudden interest in my games?

She was living rent-free in my head, and it was time for her eviction.

Jenn was smart and calculated. I had to think of the best way to approach her. Suddenly, Brian's advice popped into my head. While it wasn't a love letter, I thought a letter would be the best way to clear my head and show true contrition. I sat down to write, which I hadn't done in a long time, as my school uses laptops for everything, and words started to pour out of my pen. It forced me to realize that my handwriting was awful, truly embarrassing, but I felt it would add another layer to my ingenuity.

Jenn,

I don't know where to start. I know you're upset, and I wish you would talk to me so that I could clear things up.

I did not, nor would I ever, purposefully stand you up. I promise

I wasn't just sitting there shooting the breeze with Brooke. She just happened to walk up behind me while I was doing homework.

Pause.

I knew that was a lie, but I didn't know why I felt the need to lie. I lied, nonetheless, and I had no intentions of telling the truth. I guess "doing homework" sounded better than "working on content for my vlog." I thought she might be impressed because, apparently, impressing her was important to me.

I still wake up early and work on our packet every day.

That was not a lie. Jenn had been committed to helping me do better and learn and understand what we were working on in class and what was coming up. She was so committed that she created a workbook that covered the next two chapters. I was also honest when I told my parents I was working hard at doing better, so I got up every morning and worked so that I wouldn't fall behind again. Besides, I hadn't told my mother Jenn ended our agreement, so I needed to be up and at 'em like everything was still the same.

I'm doing okay, but I would be doing so much better if you would give me another chance. You make learning fun, even though you're mean. You make me smile, even when you yell at me. We work well together. I know you see that. I wish you would tutor me again, but even if you choose not to, at least speak to me. I hate that you're ignoring me. It makes me feel invisible. You've been telling me how smart I really am, encouraging me to believe I could do anything, and now I don't exist to you? It's weird. Anyway, I hope you find it in your heart to forgive me.

Sincerely,

Nimrod

I heard the line "I hope you find it in your heart to forgive me" on something my mom was watching. It stuck with me. I thought it best to sign the letter with "Nimrod" because it would stick with her. Once, she asked me if I knew any synonyms for the word "Hunter." Of course, I didn't. I had never thought to look it up. Well, she had, for whatever reason.

"Did you know your name was synonymous with the word 'nimrod?'" she asked, overly excited.

"No," I responded unenthusiastically.

"Do you even know what a nimrod is?" she asked with far too much joy. She was beaming from ear to ear, smiling so hard, and it made me smile.

"I don't," I said smiling, "but I'm 1000% sure that I'll know within the next 20 seconds."

"That's the best part! A nimrod is a hunter *or* an idiot!" she exclaimed as she burst into uncontrollable laughter.

My smile dissipated.

One look at my displeasure sent her further into her frenzy.

I cracked a small smile and chastised her for losing focus, a welcomed reversal of roles. She pulled herself together and picked up her pencil. As she walked toward me, I asked, "So, do you think I'm more of an idiot or more of a hunter?"

She fell to the floor in a fit of laughter. I joined her. We didn't get much done that day. It was the best day.

I realized I was smiling as I sat at my desk. At some point, Callie had found her way into my room. I looked down at her and felt happy. No, I was more than happy. I remember hearing at church that happiness was fleeting because it depended on what was happening. I did not feel mere happiness. I felt joy. It was weird. I couldn't stop smiling.

Then, Callie farted. Smile gone.

"Mom, Callie stinks," I called to my mother as I picked Callie up and put her on my lap. She looked at me and smiled; at least I think it was a smile. It could've been more gas. Smile returned.

I was determined to take this joy into the playoffs, regardless of what was happening around me, which meant I would keep this letter to myself, at least for the time being.

Chapter Fourteen

Somehow, between studying, practices, and games, Jude and I were able to upload a new video. Well, we filmed separately, and Jude edited them, so they flowed seamlessly. I wasn't that great at editing, so I left all the technical mumbo jumbo to him until I got better. I didn't see the video before he posted it, but I trusted him to deliver quality content.

I had to watch a scouting video for the upcoming final. We had won the semi-final game comfortably, thanks, in part, to my newfound joy. I floated all over the court. I passed better, I shot better, and I took my misses in stride where I'd normally beat myself up over any sign of imperfection. All around, I was a better teammate, championing all my guys. So, I was confident heading into the final game, but I knew I would be prepared, too.

I was sitting with Coach and a few other guys when I heard my phone ding. The alert was different than my normal ringtone, but I ignored it because I was focused, laser-focused. I wasn't going to let anything deter me. It dinged, again and again, followed by the familiar tone for a text message. What was going on?

I waited for Coach to reveal his plan to stop the opposing team's big man, a 13-year-old 6'2" 185-pound seventh grader. David was the tallest kid on our team. He stood at 5'11" and weighed a whopping 130 pounds… with bricks in his pockets. That's saying a lot coming from me because I'm no Santa Clause (Santa, really? The only portly figure I could come up with was Jolly Old Saint Nick. I've got to read more.) Seriously, though, he was so skinny that Cadence once told him he needed a burger. In response, he patted her on top of her head like a puppy, and she promptly kicked him in the shin.

The plan was simple enough – keep their big man out of the paint at all costs. Our weight training class was finally going to be tested. Coach also wanted us to switch to get him on a smaller man to draw fouls. I hoped I never had to switch on him. I could only imagine what running into him would feel like. I envisioned a smart car running into a brick wall, a brick wall that talked trash. The thought made my head hurt. I got up to get some water and steal a glance at my phone.

I grabbed my Hydro Flask and peeked at my phone, which had just received yet another alert. Our vlog! I sat my water down to scroll through the notifications. New comments and subscribers. It was lit! I put my phone on silent before returning to our video session.

We watched two hours of video and added 30 minutes of defensive drills. I was ready. We were ready.

I walked out of the gym, full of confidence and swag. The championship was ours. I knew it. I started my walk home and remembered I needed to check all our video interactions. I sat on a short brick wall and pulled out my phone. I was excited to see what everyone thought. I hadn't seen the video yet, but this was a great sign.

I had more than vlog notifications. I had about four new texts. I decided to wait until I got home to check them all. It was getting dark, and I hated walking in the dark. I hopped off the wall and instantly felt a sharp pain in my ankle. I grabbed it and toppled over from the weight of my backpack. This could not be happening. I tried to get myself together and stand up, but I could not put much weight on it. I had rolled my ankle enough to know it could potentially be serious.

I was worried.

I tried to calm down before I called my mom. I took a deep breath and cleared my throat.

"Hey, Mom," I responded to her rushed greeting. "It's getting kind of dark, and I don't really want to walk home. Can you or Pop please come to get me from school?"

I didn't want to tell her I was in excruciating pain. She'd immediately freak out.

"Oh, no. I wish you had called a little sooner. I'm in Henderson, running a few errands, and your dad switched with someone so that he could be at your game on Thursday."

Henderson was nearly 40 minutes away. I have to say, I was not expecting her to be unavailable. Mom was always there when I needed her. Always. I was stumped.

"Hello?" she repeated.

"I'm sorry, I'm here," I replied.

"Are you going to be okay walking? Do you need me to call your uncle?" she offered.

"No, that's okay. I'm fine," I lied. "I have to get going."

"Okay, I'm so sorry, Baby," she morosely replied. "Call me if you get too scared. We can talk the whole way home."

I hung up and reached deep into the crevices of my brain. My mom and dad usually drove me everywhere. If not them, then Granma Lou would pick me up. I wish I could call her right now. I wish she were here to talk about Brooke, Jenn, and basketball... to talk about everything. She always knew exactly what to do in every situation. I began to wonder if it was strange we had been so close or that I missed her so much. I mean, I am a teenage boy, and she was an elderly woman. I didn't care either way. She was one of my closest friends and not a day went by that I didn't think of her.

I noticed myself slipping into a daydream. I had to snap out of it and find a ride. I figured out who to call, but no part of me was interested in calling.

I scanned through my contacts for another option, but there were none. I sat on the curb, defeated, as the phone rang.

***

"You really are an idiot, ya know," Dom teased as he helped me to my feet. "You're lucky practice was over. You barely caught me."

"I really appreciate it, Dominic," I confessed.

"*Dominic?* It's Dom, or D, even 'Nic, but never *Dominic*. Got it, punk?" he questioned.

I understood though I would never call him D or Nic.

He yammered on about how tough practice had been, how he hoped for a scholarship, and how he couldn't wait to get away from his parents and Brooke, especially now that she was dating Brian.

I drowned him out. I was so worried about my ankle that everything else was background noise.

What if it was sprained?

What if I couldn't play on Thursday?

My parents told me not to play "What If," that it was a dangerous game, and the more I played, the more likely I was to lose. I didn't want to give in to negative thoughts. The past few days had been too perfect. I wasn't ready to give that up.

Dom got me home without incident (no speeding or no screaming at old ladies), helped me inside, and got an icepack out of the freezer. He was nice again. He told me that he had a lot going on and just needed someone to talk to. Apparently, I was that someone. Since I had tuned him out, I had no idea I had been a listening ear. I guess you never know what someone is going through.

"Rice," he yelled as he headed toward the door.

"What?" I replied, completely confused.

"R.I.C.E. You know: Rest, Ice, Compress, Elevate," he explained. "Your team needs you. B told me you are a little baller. She said she likes to watch you play, which must mean something because she hates basketball."

"Yeah, she's been coming to the games. I've been helping her understand what's going on. I didn't realize I was the reason for her sudden interest in basketball."

"Not you, you nimrod. I already told you why," he insulted.

I laughed, remembering what nimrod meant.

"Okay, whatever. I just hope my ankle isn't injured too bad," I admitted.

"It should be cool. I broke my ankle once, remember? It was way worse than this. I'm out. Be careful," he screamed as he walked out of the door.

I did remember. When Brooke and I were ten, the three of us were playing an intense game of tag at the park. Leading up to that point, Brooke had been taller and faster than me. However, I was in the middle of a growth spurt. I had grown much taller than her and was determined to prove I was faster, too. Dom was chasing us. I was running super fast. In my head, I was running at the speed of light. I knew I was dusting B. I looked to my left, nowhere in sight. I turned to my right, and there she was, smiling brightly. I couldn't help but laugh. We were having so much fun, running and laughing, until Dom's foot got stuck in a little hole and he hurt his ankle. I didn't realize until now that he had actually broken it. I remember him crying about missing basketball games. I held his hand, and he called me his little brother. He was 13 at the time, my age now. I had completely forgotten about that day.

Chapter Fifteen

My mother was absolutely inconsolable when she realized why I needed a ride.

"Why didn't you tell me you hurt yourself?" she cried. "I'm a horrible mother. I should've been there."

"It's okay, Mom," I comforted her. "Really, it was good that Dom picked me up. We were able to catch up."

"Doesn't matter," she ignored me, "I should've heard it in your voice."

"Relax. You don't have Spidey senses or anything. Give yourself a break."

She looked at me with despondent eyes. She was really sad, and that was crazy to me. How could she be sad because I was hurt?

"Let me look at it," she said as she gingerly lifted my injured ankle. "It doesn't look that bad, but let's go see Dr. Williams. I'll call right now."

Cadence had been standing there, quiet as a mouse.

"Cay, are you okay?" I asked.

Tears welled in her eyes as she nodded her head. She grabbed my hand tightly—my little monster.

I tried to stand up. It wasn't as bad as it had been earlier, but it still hurt a lot. Cadence reached out her free hand as if to catch me. I sat back down and motioned for her to sit next to me. She looked at my leg and shook her head. She wasn't sure what was hurting, and she didn't want to make it worse.

Mom walked over to me with the phone to her ear.

"What happened?" she asked.

"I was sitting on a short wall, and I wasn't really paying attention when I stepped down, and I think I rolled my ankle," I retold the story.

Mom repeated everything I said into her phone.

"Dr. Williams asked if you turned it or rolled it."

"I probably turned it," I answered. I didn't know the difference. Turned, rolled, all I know is that it hurt, and I didn't want to answer any more questions.

"He thinks he turned it," she told Dr. Williams. "Can you see him today?"

She listened for three minutes before she responded with a mere "okay" and ended the call.

I watched her as she started cleaning up the living room, saying nothing at all. She was a bit of a neat freak, but to be cleaning at this moment was absurd.

"Uh, Mom," I interrupted, "What did he say?"

"Oh, I'm sorry, Baby. He doesn't think he'll be able to see you today. It's really busy in his office."

It was like a gut punch. I needed to know if I could play.

She must've seen the dejected look on my face because she grabbed the hand that Cadence was holding and softly said, "He's going to FaceTime us in five minutes. He'll look at it and tell us if we should go to the hospital."

I relaxed into the pillows on the couch, and Cadence sat next to me. We waited, holding hands the whole time. My palm started sweating, but she wouldn't let go. I tried pulling it away, but she wasn't having it.

Mom's phone rang, and my heart started beating ultra fast. I really wanted everything to be okay. No, I *needed* everything to be okay.

"Hi, Dr. Williams," I crooned as I saw my pediatrician's chubby face. "How are you today?" I asked.

I wasn't interested in how he was doing. It was merely a platitude my mother insisted I include with most greetings. It just spewed out of my mouth. She's got me trained like a puppy, that woman.

"I'm well, young Daniel Son," he chuckled.

I had never seen the original *Karate Kid* movie, only the remake, but older people always made this silly joke. They either called me Daniel Son, or they'd say, "Wax on, wax off." I had to search the internet to figure out what they were talking about. Apparently, Daniel was the student, and adding the "son" was a respect thing. I wasn't exactly sure, but that's what I surmised.

"Now, let's take a look at that ankle," he said as he looked over the rim of his glasses.

I grabbed the phone and showed him my swollen ankle.

"I see," he hummed. "No deformities or bruising. Is it throbbing?"

"No, no throbbing. Is that a good thing?" my eyes grew big.

"Hold your horses. Let's get through this the right way," he instructed. "Let me see your other leg," he said as I moved my other leg into the camera of the phone. "Okay, I see swelling. Does it hurt when you touch it?"

"I haven't touched it," I blurted.

I hated to admit it, but I have a very, very, *very* low tolerance for pain. Everything hurt! A basketball bounced off my head in practice; it hurt. I fell off my bike; it hurt. Someone jokingly punched me in the arm; yes, it hurt, so you can imagine what I was going through with this ankle situation – a whole lot of hurt. Touching my already hurt ankle was the furthest thing from my mind.

"I need you to press lightly around the swollen area. Gentle but firm," he directed.

Gentle but firm? How does one accomplish such a feat?

"Mom, can you gently touch my ankle firmly?" I teased.

"Stop being difficult, Hunter," she said sternly.

Once again, Mom examined my ankle. While I held the camera, she used her pointer finger to attack my tender flesh firmly.

"Hey! What happened to gentle?" I screamed. "You went full firm. Those were not the rules."

I pulled my ankle away and did as the doctor asked. After a quick self-examination, Dr. Williams determined there was no break. He didn't even think there was a sprain.

"R.I.C.E," he instructed. "You should be fine to play this week, but no practice tomorrow."

"Doc, my middle school thanks you," I bowed to the phone.

"Uh, I did nothing. Good luck."

"So, you're okay?" Cadence implored.

"Yes, I'm fine—no break or tear. So lucky," I cheered.

"Not lucky, blessed," Mom chimed in.

"Aw, man, you're just a baby," Cadence exclaimed. "A big teenage baby! I'm going to tell all of your friends."

She hopped off the couch and tried to pick up Callie. Callie protested by throwing up. Cadence, unwilling to clean anything, looked to see if Mom saw and slowly walked away—such a monster.

Crisis averted. I was going to R.I.C.E. the heck out of my ankle. Recovery was all that mattered. Tomorrow was a different story.

Chapter Sixteen

After getting off the phone with Dr. Williams, I called Coach. I heard the joy dissipate from his voice as I explained what happened. It was clear he was disappointed but wanted what was best for me, so he insisted I would not be allowed to practice until the morning of the game – *if* I passed his health assessment. Coach is no doctor, but he knew a lot about sports injuries. He always astounded me in STEM with his wealth of knowledge. He seemed to know a lot about everything.

It was Monday, and to think I couldn't practice for two whole days leading up to the most important game of my life was soul-shattering. I would have to fill that time not to go crazy.

Just then, I remembered all the alerts and texts from earlier. It was the perfect time to watch our newest video and respond to the feedback.

Mom did her absolute best to help me upstairs and into bed. I had decided to settle in for the night. I was too nervous or anxious to eat, so I got comfortable in bed, opened my laptop, and went straight to our channel.

Our latest videos were our most viewed yet. It also boasted the most comments, a mere six interactions, but that tripled our high of two. I went straight to the comments section. The first comment was a lot of emojis, mainly laughing faces. I tend to think I'm pretty funny, so I skimmed past it, hoping to get to more meaningful contributions.

The next comment was a bit confusing, so I went directly to the comment that followed. I was even more lost.

B@llerBoi23 wrote, "Hunt UR crazy. Why would you post that?"

I had made some controversial NBA playoff picks, but I didn't think they were so outlandish to receive that kind of feedback.

The next comment: "Yo! No way that's to who I think it is. Hunt, what were you thinking? Keep that to urself, bro."

I had no clue what he was talking about, so I scrolled up to the video's description for insight.

No help.

I felt like I was working backward, so I watched the video.

It started the same as all our videos: our crazy intro, and then Jude edited footage of me playing and fused it with a video of him live streaming Fortnite. I don't know how he did it, but people loved it. I watched with pride as my skills were on full display. The video then transitioned into my playoff spiel, which was a pleasant surprise because he usually showcased his gaming first.

I listened as I explained why I thought the worst team in the league still had a shot at the playoffs, but I directed my attention to my phone. I knew what I said, and I knew how I looked. I listened to see if he added any commentary or changed my sequencing.

I had a lot of texts from a number I didn't know, in addition to texts from most of my friends. Maybe Dom had told someone what happened to me.

As I read the unknown text, I heard my voice on the computer creep to a slow drawl. I looked at the screen, expecting to see my face all screwed up. Jude played a lot of games and pranked us all the time. I figured he took an opportunity to prank me since I hadn't seen the video before it was posted. What I found left me completely flabbergasted.

I jumped out of bed, forgetting about my ankle, and grabbed my backpack. I searched frantically, to no avail. I dumped everything out of my bag and scrambled through its contents; it had to be there. I searched my folder, my desk, under my bed – nothing. It was nowhere to be found. I already knew where it was. I already knew who possessed it. I already knew, and as shocked as I wanted to be, I was not at all surprised.

On display for everyone to laugh at and pick apart was my letter to Jenn. I don't know how Jude got it, but there it was, in all its glory. I was more angry than embarrassed. But more than anything, my feelings were hurt.

They use everything against you.

I knew this to be a fact, so I shouldn't have been hurt, but I was.

I returned to the unknown texts. In sequential order, they read:

I do not forgive you.

I will never forgive you.

Ask Brooke for help.

You are invisible to me.

I stared at the computer screen. I knew they were there, but I couldn't see the words of my letter which was superimposed over my face.

As if I needed to snap back to reality, my ankle started to throb, but I didn't need any jolts. I was present. I was there, in the moment, and I didn't know what to do next.

I laid back and elevated my leg.

R.I.C.E.

My phone dinged yet again. I looked reluctantly. It was Dom. Maybe he was still in an inspirational mood:

Hey. Don't say anything about Brooke dating Brian to anyone.

I wasn't supposed to say anything.

She'll kill me.

Had he told me that? In my injured haze, had I missed such important news?

It was the final punch to the gut. I fell back into my pillows.

R.I.C.E.

Chapter Seventeen

I tried to sleep. I wanted more than anything to forget the avalanche of disaster that descended over my life after practice. I needed a "forget me stick" to erase six hours of my life.

Unfortunately, like an elephant, I remembered. Every excruciating detail was stored in my memory bank. I could already see my older self withdrawing this information to impart wisdom to my future nieces and nephews. Stories of this day would serve as a warning for them, cautionary tales of fake friends and real foes.

The day was simply a lot to digest. I didn't know where to start. One thing was certain – sleep would not hinder the unraveling chaos that was my life. Sleep, while deeply sought after, was playing hard to get.

I decided not to look at the comments, not to check my text messages. I ignored them all. Out of sight, out of mind, right? Wrong. I ignored them in the physical, but they danced around my mind all night long.

One thing I knew I couldn't ignore… Jude. I'd have to talk to him. As much as I'd like *him* to be invisible, he was very much present and the source of most of today's misery. I'd have to deal with him, even though he'd just call it a joke and laugh it off. Only it wasn't funny. So far, none of the comments or texts involved anyone laughing at me, but the entire situation was evil. Okay, evil is a bit much. It was savage, uncivilized.

I never understood how people could be so cruel. My whole life turned upside down and not just mine. Jude dragged Jenn and Brooke into it, too.

Aw, man, Brooke. I completely forgot about Brooke. Her name was barely mentioned in the letter. I didn't think it would be that big of a deal, but Dom's bomb was like Hiroshima. How could she date Brian of all people? I couldn't wrap my head around it. We were having so much fun together.

How could she like another boy? Meanwhile, Jenn was never going to speak to me again. My life was a train wreck. I didn't even know to press the brake.

Everything was a complete mess, and I didn't have anyone to vent to. I'd always held everyone at a distance to avoid this very thing, and it seemed not talking to anyone was hurting more than helping. All my theories were wrong; my whole playbook was out the window— a fantastic collision.

***

I woke up to a massive headache and a throbbing foot. I didn't remember falling asleep, but I was grateful for the intermission.

What time was it? I reached for my phone. There was a faint light peeking through my blackout curtains, so I figured it was nearing daytime. I heard my phone drop to the floor as I groped in the semi-darkness. Two things I knew for sure – one, I wasn't getting up to find my phone. I didn't want to see what was on it anyway, and two, I wasn't going to school, so I didn't need to know what time it was anyway.

The second revelation was comforting. Delayed confrontations were one of my favorite types of confrontations. The only confrontation better than delayed was one that doesn't happen at all. Since the latter wasn't an option, I took solace in my small victory, closed my eyes, and dozed off.

I had another weird dream: there was a fire in my room. Dad stood there in turnout gear, watching as the fire burned, making sure the flames didn't spread to the rest of the house. I was so upset. All my things were being ruined, and he didn't seem to care.

"We taught you to prevent fires. You get upset with us for trying to help, so you have to put it out yourself," he yelled over the intense crackling of the blaze.

"Besides," Mom chimed in from downstairs, "There really isn't anything of value in there. You haven't truly connected with any of it."

I watched her return to her cleaning. She was dusting pictures of me, making sure they weren't covered in ash. There were no pictures of Cadence, only me. There were so many pictures, I couldn't count them, and she made sure every one was pristine.

As Dad watched my room intently, he gestured toward the corner where he had left a large fire extinguisher. I turned toward him helplessly. Catching a glimpse of myself in the hallway mirror, I noticed I was dressed in full turnout gear as well. I took a deep breath. I knew what I had to do, but I was scared. I tried to summon courage, but it wasn't there. The house started to tremble. I thought it was going to collapse. I heard Mom's voice, but it was distant. She was repeating the same thing over and over, but I couldn't make it out. All of a sudden, I heard her holler loud and clear, "Get up!"

I slowly opened my eyes.

Mom was standing over me in her robe, shaking my shoulders. I thought it might be a dream within a dream until I heard her exclaim, "Hunter Daniel Stevens, if you don't get out of this bed and get ready for school!"

That was the real Mom. Dream Mom was much nicer.

"Wha?" I managed to murmur. "I have to go to school?"

"Yes, you have to go to school," she countered. "You aren't sick. You aren't severely injured. Dr.

Williams suggested I get you an air cast to help with mobility. Here, try this on."

She handed me a plastic brace. It looked like it was lined in bubble wrap.

"He said it would help you walk around while keeping it compressed and safe. He also said you were cleared to go to school, so get up!"

Was Dr. Williams trying to ruin my life?

"Mom," I cooed, "It really hurts. Walking on it will definitely make it worse."

I tilted my head and looked deep into her eyes. I searched her soul for any sign of empathy.

"Your dad told me not to let you smooth talk your way out of school," she replied as she casually crushed my spirit. "You're going. Period. Do you want me to pull the crutches out of the shed?"

"No," I answered in defeat.

I secured the straps around the cast and stood to my feet. It hurt, but not that much.

I winced in pain, more of a show for my mom. She was unphased as she moved toward the door. She knew all my tricks, and she wasn't having it.

Sigh.

Callie strolled into the room as if to inquire about the commotion. She beelined for the cast, sniffing it profusely. Satisfied that it wasn't dangerous, she looked at me with worry in her eyes.

"I'm okay," I admitted.

"Are you really?" a tiny voice asked from outside of my room.

"Yes, Cay," I comforted my sister. "I really am okay. I promise."

As she peeked her ponytails through the doorway, I could see she was still anxious.

"Cadence, I pinky swear I'm fine. Can you be strong for me? It's hard for me to get better knowing you're so concerned."

"No," she stated plainly. "I can't be strong. I'm only eight. Can you be strong? Can you be strong for both of us?"

"I can try," I whispered sheepishly.

"No, brother, don't try," she demanded, "Do!"

I could see she was serious. She needed me, and I would be there for her.

"Yes, Cay. I will be strong for both of us, I pinky promise," I proclaimed with confidence.

"Good," she nodded, gently hugging my leg before walking into her room to get ready for school.

That was all she needed. It was all I needed.

Chapter Eighteen

It wasn't as easy to maneuver as Mom and Dr. Williams had claimed, but I was able to get dressed and hobble out of the door without incident.

In the car, Mom asked if I was okay about 20 times.

"I know you may be in a little pain, but you seem totally distracted," Mom explained. "You seem zombie-fied."

"I'm just worried about the championship game," I lied.

Yes, the game was back there somewhere, but front and center in my mind was the vlog and infamous letter. I was nearly trembling, thinking of what was in store for me at school.

Cadence had asked if she could be dropped off after me. I felt like she was being a drama queen. I mean, who was hurt anyway?

As I was stepping out of the car, Cadence asked, "Who's the best boy?"

I stopped dead in my tracks. Had I heard her correctly? Maybe I was hearing things again.

Before I had the chance to ask her to repeat herself, she echoed, "Who's the best boy?"

Her tone, her pronunciation, everything about the way she spoke was exactly as Granma Lou had asked about a hundred times.

I smiled and turned toward Cadence.

"I am," I replied confidently.

"Are you going to be happy and strong?" she asked—another Granma reference.

"I will be happy and strong, for you and me."

"Be extra strong for you," she demanded.

"Whatever you say, boss," I said and winked as I got out of the car.

I watched my mom reach back and try to hug Cay. Tears streamed down her face. I thought she might be thinking of what an amazing woman

Granma Lou was, or maybe she was thinking that Cadence was an amazing kid. Either way, they were both true.

Cay had stepped in where no one else had been able. I was holding so tightly to Granma's memory that I hadn't realized I wasn't allowing anyone else to reach me. I heard my parents and obeyed them, but I hadn't been truly listening. I had unknowingly cut off my mom and dad and with them went my confidence and trust. Losing Granma had been painful. I didn't want to ever go through that again, so I refused to let anyone in. Even the people that cared about me the most.

Honestly, I hadn't felt like the "best boy" for a while.

I can't believe I was sitting outside of school having this huge ah-ha moment. I've always felt a little awkward because my grandmother and I were so close. My friends had made it very clear that hanging out with old people was not cool. Not to mention, this whole moment felt like a kids' special on TV. You know, where the kid has this huge revelation and everything falls into place afterward?

I shook off those thoughts and limped onto campus. TV special or not, I did feel more confident. I wasn't sure what I'd say to Jude. Hopefully, the words would come to me by the time I saw him, but I was done with being scared.

It was déjà vu. All eyes were on me, once again. People approached me with a wide array of questions.

"What happened to your leg?"

"Are you going to be able to play on Thursday?"

"Does the team know?"

It never occurred to me that people would be more concerned with my injury than my drama.

I answered every question with a smile, realizing my team didn't know, and they'd be super bummed.

I was feeling a little better until the inevitable, "So, did she forgive you?"

It was like a chain reaction, a domino effect. Everyone who spoke to me after that point mentioned Jenn or the letter.

I tried to look on the bright side – our vlog must have had tons of views – but even the bright side was dim because the Bucket Bros were officially dead. I waited so long for a channel, and Jude ruined it. The more I thought about it, I was really mad at him. This was all his fault. Well, not my ankle, or Brooke and Brian, but I would take it all out on him.

I had let it stew. I was ready for this confrontation. I couldn't wait to see him. I was going to let him have it. I had to set an example for future instigators. Hunter Stevens was off-limits.

Shuffling toward first period, I went over my monologue in my head:

"What kind of friend are you?"

"You really think you're funny?! You're a clown."

"Why did Jenn deserve this?"

"Everything is a joke to you?"

"You play too much."

"You went too far, Jude."

I would show him that his actions had consequences, and we would never be friends again.

I sauntered into STEM class, admittedly dejected. I knew Coach would be let down, which made me sad. I guess this is how Mom feels sometimes. I looked at my air cast before I walked into class. I was going to be okay, and I was going to play. I kept repeating that in my head. I looked up, and the whole team was standing around Coach's desk, including Jude.

"What's going on here?" I probed.

Coach stood up and walked toward me. Gently placing his hand on my shoulder, he replied, "You sounded down on the phone. I wanted to cheer you up. We all have your back, no matter what."

I looked at the team. Jude's head was hung low, and our power forward, Kyle, pushed him into the desk.

"Thanks," I muttered, "but I don't know if *everyone* really cares."

"Jude is stupid," Will, a.k.a. B@llerBoi23, added.

"Yeah," the team chorused.

Things were feeling TV movie-ish again.

Will must've felt the same because he asked if they could go back to class. As they piled out, I stared Jude down, burning a hole in his soul. He was laughing with another teammate until we made eye contact. He quickly looked away and rushed out.

Class was normal. We created a cube puzzle. I worked quietly, which I realized was far more efficient, but quiet was boring. I knew it wouldn't last.

I ran into Mrs. Lattimore on the way to my next class.

"Aw, poor baby," she called out.

"I'm really okay, Mrs. L," I responded. "It isn't anything major. I plan to play on Thursday."

"Well, you make sure you're healed before you step on the court," she advised. "We need you, but not at the expense of your health."

"Yes, ma'am."

Every adult said the same thing. They must have some kind of script they rehearse for moments like this.

"Take care of yourself. There will be more championship games," was my Dad's motivational speech.

Jenn wasn't in math class. She wasn't in school at all. I felt terrible.

Jude avoided me the entire lunch period. I couldn't chase him down, so I let it go. I knew I would see him eventually, and he would have to listen.

No one gave me too hard of a time, either. Maybe it was the injury, or maybe middle school kids aren't as bad as I thought.

I decided to go to the bathroom before class. It took me forever to get anywhere. What if I had to pee and couldn't get there fast enough? Could you imagine the uproar I'd make if I peed on myself? Yeah, I needed to find a toilet quickly.

I stumbled into the bathroom by the cafeteria, and who did I see scrolling on his phone? None other than jokester Jude.

I took a deep breath and bellowed, "I thought you were my boy."

That was it. All the mental rehearsing and monologuing. All the anger and pain. Everything that I was going through and planned to take out on him and all I could express was disappointment.

"I'm sorry, man," he whimpered. "I thought it would be funny. It turns out, it was more embarrassing than anything else."

He admitted to finding the letter when he was looking for a pen a few days ago.

"I didn't think it would upset you or Jenn. I took it too far," he admitted. "I understand if you don't want to do BB anymore."

I was shocked. He pretty much covered everything. I wanted to scream at him, but I could tell that he was genuinely sorry.

"Why didn't you say all of that this morning?" I asked. It would have been much more satisfying if he had apologized in front of everyone.

"Man, the guys were so mean this morning. They called me all types of names after I told them that I posted the letter. I thought they would laugh – they didn't. Why do you think I'm in here? They said they didn't want to kick it with me until I apologized."

More shock.

"So why didn't you just apologize?"

"I was afraid you would say you didn't want to be my friend anymore," he answered honestly.

"I was going to say that," I confessed. "I didn't want anything to do with you. Jenn hates me now, even more so. You really embarrassed her."

"I know," he sulked. "I've been looking for her all day, too."

"So, everything is supposed to be fine now? You're sorry, and everything should go back to normal?"

"Well, after my post, I thought you would consider us even," he said.

The bell rang, but I wasn't finished talking. More importantly, I hadn't peed.

"What post?" I questioned.

"I text you. I said I was sorry and told you to watch the newest video on our channel."

I reached in my pocket for my phone, nothing there. I patted all my pockets, no phone. I hadn't had it all day. It was still under my bed.

"Look, I gotta go to class, Hunt," he interrupted. "I really am sorry, bro."

He left me alone by the sink.

I washed my hands. I don't know why, but I hadn't gone to the bathroom.

As I walked to class, I realized I made a lot of assumptions about Jude, and they were mostly wrong. Normally, I hated being wrong, but this wasn't so bad.

Chapter Nineteen

I slowly walked to class, mulling over everything Jude said. I was relieved he was apologetic and realized he had gone too far. While I had accepted his apology, I didn't think we could be friends anymore. I didn't think I could ever trust him again.

Since I was already late, I took my time getting to class—no need to rush to be early-late.

I peeked into several classrooms on my way. As I crept past Mrs. Chapman's Spanish class, I caught a glimpse of Brooke. My heart skipped a beat. In all of this, she had been more of an afterthought, but just a glimpse of her reminded me why she was my forever crush.

Feeling a bit giddy, I turned my thoughts to Brooke as I headed to class. My happy feelings were immediately replaced with feelings of rejection as I remembered Dom's revelation. I clearly understood why Brian liked her. She was breathtaking. I suppose I realize why she liked him as well. I always admired him. He was a really nice guy.

What was happening?

Was I excusing this torrid coupling?

How could I be okay with Brian stealing my girl?

A sudden tap on my shoulder shook me out of my thoughts. Clumsily, I turned around. Brooke stood there, lip gloss popping and curls bouncing. My heart sang.

"Why would you mention me in your letter, Hunt?" she questioned.

My thoughts were jumbled. She was visibly angry. I didn't think she would be so upset.

"Hey, B," I sang. "Where did you come from?"

"I don't have time to play with you," she quipped. Her tone was different. There was something very cutting behind each word.

"Sorry," I apologized. "I was just saying hi."

"I don't care about your hi," she replied nastily. "I'm trying to figure out why you would involve me in your drama with that nerd. You like nerds, that's fine, write them love letters all day, but keep my name out of it."

"She's not a nerd, Brooke," I said, quite assertively. "I don't know why you're being so mean. I didn't even say anything about you."

"Wow, defensive much?" she teased.

"Whatever," I mumbled.

I didn't know what else to say. I was defensive. Brooke was being ugly, and Jenn didn't deserve to be called names. No one did, especially not Jenn. She was a sweetheart, she never hurt anyone, and she deserved better.

"Is she your girlfriend?" she asked.

The question caught me off guard. Is that what people thought?

"Absolutely not," I exclaimed. "She's my tutor. I didn't want her to stop tutoring me. I have to pass math."

It seemed dirty coming out of my mouth. Calling Jenn my tutor seemed to take away from our friendship. Secretly, I didn't want Brooke or anyone else to make fun of me for hanging out with Jenn the way they made fun of me for hanging out with Granma Lou.

Suddenly, I realized I was being just as ugly as Brooke.

"Okay, I see now," Brooke replied with a renewed tone. "I knew it had to be something."

"What is that supposed to mean?"

"You needed her. I get it. I sometimes talk to nobodies to help with my homework or get lunch money. Your letter makes sense."

Lunch money? Nobodies? I was heartbroken. I cracked a fake smile and started to head toward class, feeling dejected.

"Are you going to play on Thursday?" she called after me.

She never asked if I was okay. She didn't even notice the change in my behavior. I kept walking. I didn't answer. I doubt she really cared.

***

I wasn't allowed to do anything at practice. I couldn't shoot, I couldn't dribble, I couldn't even stand. I had to sit, watch, and ice. It was cruel and unusual punishment.

Sit, watch, think. Think, watch, sit.

It was as if I was sentenced to solitary confinement of the mind. My thoughts and I had too much time together.

As directed, I sat, and I thought. I thought about school, I thought about friends, and I thought about family. Mainly, I thought about basketball, Brooke, and Jenn.

I was now completely confident that I'd be able to play on Thursday. My ankle was already better than it was when I woke up that morning. Another day and I'd be good to go. As I watched the team runs plays, I reviewed my role in my head. Defensively and offensively, I'd be ready for whatever the game brought. I was clocked in. I wish the same could be said about the girls in my life.

I was more lost than ever when it came to girls, and that's saying a lot because I knew next to nothing about them. Brooke had been so mean. It made me question why I ever liked her in the first place. Maybe Dom was right; she was a mean girl, and I didn't want to see it. If that was true, I wanted nothing to do with her, but was I like her? That was the million-dollar question.

Not wanting to think about them anymore, I pulled my laptop out of my backpack, intending to start homework. I would get everything done during practice and hopefully be able to relax at home. Maybe I could finally finish my favorite show, *Zombie High*. I started episode five a while ago, and I hadn't been able to finish it.

I logged into the school portal when I received an email notification: more vlog responses, which reminded me that Jude mentioned a new post he wanted me to check out. Without delay, I headed straight to the now-defunct Bucket Brothers channel.

Much to my surprise, the post with Jenn's letter was gone. In its place was a one-minute video, "Confessions of a Jerk."

This should be good. I got comfortable in my seat, inched closer toward the laptop, and clicked play.

The video started abruptly. Jude was sitting outside of the library looking pretty sad. I smiled. I felt bad about it, but his pain made me feel better.

"I messed up," he started. "Everyone saw the video, so there's no need for me to describe it. I thought it would be funny, but it wasn't. It was mean. All of my friends are mad at me, which isn't new, but I'm worried that my best friend will stop talking to me."

I was Jude's best friend? I never knew that. I guess guys don't talk about that kind of stuff.

Wait a minute, was Jude *my* best friend? I'd never thought of that. I'd never had a best friend. Maybe that's why I felt so betrayed.

"So, in an effort to regain his trust, I'm going to admit the most embarrassing secret in the world."

I was completely intrigued.

"One day," he began, far too slow for my liking, "I was in science class, and everyone had already left. I saw Brandon in the corner, getting something out of his backpack. I tiptoed over to him as quietly as I could. I was going to scare the life out of him."

I had no idea where this story was going, but it was taking too long to get there.

"So, I got really close and screamed in his ear, except it wasn't Brandon. It was Mr. Caldwell, the science teacher. I scared him so bad. He turned around and jumped. He actually almost hit me, but he caught himself. I think he scared me more than I scared him because I screamed like a baby and then…"

He paused for entirely too long. I leaned in closer to the computer to make sure I heard every word.

Taking a deep breath, he finished his story with the last four words I expected to hear:

"I peed on myself."

I laughed out loud, not so much because he had an accident, but because I hoped to avoid the same fate when I ran into him earlier. How ironic?

"It wasn't a little pee, either. It was like a puddle," he continued. "Once I started, I couldn't turn it off. Mr. Caldwell called my parents. I had to clean it up myself, and I had to walk around for the remainder of the day in my wet pants."

What made it even funnier was that I remembered that day very well. Jude said he spilled soda on himself, and he threw his clothes away after practice.

"I still can't look Mr. Caldwell in the eyes."

I watched as Jude shook his head before turning off the camera.

That was embarrassing, especially among 13-year-olds. Jude's admission far surpassed my measly six comments, bringing in 24 comments and counting. The views kept climbing, too. There was no way I could abandon BB after all of this new traffic.

I would let Jude sweat a little, but I decided I wouldn't abandon him, either. After all, best friends go through things, right?

I think he learned his lesson, but I was still learning mine.

Chapter Twenty

The next few days crept by slowly. I was not practicing, but I was using my downtime to study film. Dad finished his shift and was in full-blown coach-mode. The family room had been transformed into a basketball command center.

I was so focused on the game that I managed to put Brooke and Jenn out of my mind. Outside of family ties, I was pretty much done with Brooke. She'd still be around, and I was okay with that, but any feelings for her were left in the hallway of the language building.

The night before the game, I said a special prayer. Cay and Callie joined me. We prayed that my hands would be blessed, and win or lose, I wouldn't cry.

Among family, I was known to be a crier, another secret I would never tell anyone at school.

Cadence had turned into my little warrior, but she'd always be my monster.

Mom made a huge breakfast on the morning of the game. Normally, nerves kept me from enjoying food on game days, but I stuffed my face today. Syrup dripped from my chin onto my shirt, but I didn't care. Nothing could change my mood.

Dad gave me a fist bump as he dropped me off at school.

"I'll see you at the game," he said. "And no matter what –."

"I'm a champion in your eyes," I interrupted.

"I was going to say that no matter what, don't let anyone tell you syrup and ketchup on your shirt isn't cool," he laughed.

I looked down at my shirt. There was a huge ketchup stain right under the syrup drizzle. After my latest debacle, I tried hard not to draw attention to myself at school. This was the opposite. Oh, well. The show must go on.

There were still a few whispers as I walked around campus. Jude had managed to bring more attention to the entire situation with his admission post, but it wasn't that bad. Jenn avoiding me was the worst of it.

Surprisingly, teachers were taking it easy with assignments because of the game. It was the first time the school had made it to the championship... ever. It was a pretty big deal for everyone.

With the school day flying by, I was growing more excited as the hours passed. By the time the bell rang after my last class, I was nearly bouncing off the walls. I could not contain my enthusiasm.

The game was being played on neutral ground at Wilson High. Since Wilson was about 15 minutes away, we were taking the school bus to the game. Everyone had to be at the bus by 2:55 p.m. Coach was very serious when he gave us our directions for departure.

"The bus is leaving the lot at 3 p.m. sharp," he exclaimed. "If you're not on the bus, you're not playing in the game. Plain and simple." His tone made it very clear that he would leave anyone who wasn't on that bus.

I didn't want to risk it, so I started toward the bus lot at 2:45 p.m. School had been out for 15 minutes. I figured I'd have ten minutes to try and calm myself. Admittedly, I was a bit too excited.

I fixed my eyes on the bus and marched forward, like a soldier heading to war. I don't think I had ever been more focused in my entire life. This game was mine for the taking.

Marching ahead, I must have had tunnel vision on the bus because I did not see the hurdle coming straight for me.

"I understand we weren't exactly friends, but I didn't know you were using me."

Jenn stood in front of me with tears in her eyes.

"Huh?" I replied, completely lost.

"Brooke is going around telling everyone that you only wrote the letter because you didn't want me to stop tutoring you. She said you told her that we weren't friends, that you needed me to pass math, and then you'd be done with me."

I was dumbfounded. Brooke was officially a mean girl.

"Jenn, I promise, I didn't say that. I would never say that," I said frantically.

"So, she just made it up? Why would she?" she asked.

I didn't know. I didn't care. She was dead wrong, but I was done letting her control me. I would make this right, despite her.

"Honestly, I don't know why, but I do know that you are my friend before you are my tutor. That's why I wrote the letter. I don't want to lose your friendship. I've learned a lot about friendship during this whole ordeal and I realize that you are one of my best friends."

The words shocked me when they came out of my mouth, but they were true. Jenn was my best friend. They must have shocked her, too, because Jenn sat there silent for a whole minute.

The team started arriving to the bus. Everyone watched intently as I continued.

"Between Jude's post and Brooke's lies, the universe doesn't seem to want us to be friends, but we have fun together, and I don't ever listen to the universe."

She laughed. That was a good sign.

"Don't make me laugh," she said sternly. "I'm mad at you. You are the worst friend. I've never had so much drama in my life."

"And I'm sorry, I'm so sorry, but friends go through things. Ask Jude."

"They do," Jude chimed in from the bus.

"Shut up, Jude," I heard someone yell. I think it was Will. He was turning out to be a great ally. A friend, even.

"Yes," Jenn added. "Shut. Up. Jude. You've caused enough trouble."

I smiled. That was the Jenn I knew.

"What are you smiling at? You are not out of the woods," she said as she stomped her feet.

"I hate to disturb this soap opera," Coach interrupted. "but it's 2:59 p.m., and you are not actually on the bus."

I panicked.

"Jenn, I have to go. Will you please come to the game?" I begged.

I was standing in the doorway of the bus, pleading.

"Please? Pretty please with a cherry on top?"

"No," she casually replied, looking at her nails.

I got down on my knees. Coach promptly pulled me up.

"Boy, get off your knees. You need them for the game," Coach remarked. "The door is closing. Are you on or off?"

"On," I replied as I ran to my seat.

Opening the window, I called out to Jenn.

"Will you be there?"

"I will not be there. I have a previous engagement," she answered.

I slumped down in my seat as the bus pulled out of the lot. Everyone was laughing, but not in a mean way. It was kind of brotherly like I'd do to Cay.

Kyle patted me on my back.

"Girls are nothing but trouble," he sighed.

He was right. I had been in such a great mood, and now I felt completely defeated. I felt pretty dumb. How could I let her get to me like this? I crossed my arms and put my head into my lap. I spent the entire bus ride trying to get my mind right. It didn't work.

I sulked to the locker room. I put my uniform on in a cloud of sadness. I grabbed my phone. I always put it on silent before games so it wouldn't disturb me.

One unknown text.

It was Jenn.

I'll be at your stupid game.

My face brightened. I responded with a smiley face emoji. My heart was happy.

Coach called for a huddle before we went onto the court.

"We've worked hard to get here. Let's show everyone we deserve it just as much as anyone else. The score is zero to zero, even playing field. Let's run it up!"

"Run it up," Will yelled as we all placed our hands in the middle of the huddle.

"Run it up," we screamed in unison.

We walked out of the locker room, chanting that same phrase over and over.

I was ready.

We were ready.

Chapter Twenty-One

By halftime, we were up by 12 points. I had nine points, three rebounds, and one steal. Mom had been warned by the referees twice, and Cadence had yelled at me four times.

I hadn't seen Jenn, but I wasn't exactly looking for her. It had been harder than I thought to contain their shooting guard. He scored on me twice. I didn't like that, so I focused on defense more than I ever had in my life.

Coach's voice was calm at halftime, but we could see he was fired up. We fed off of his energy.

At the end of the third, our lead was only four, and we were visibly rattled. Coach never lost his cool, but we were all losing it.

"Basketball is a game of runs. They had their run, now it's our turn," Coach lamented during a time out.

We went up by another four points. Then they went on a 10-0 run.

We were panicking.

Dad came over to the bench. His face was full of concern. I assured him with a simple head nod. He taught me to put out my own fires. He returned the nod and went back to his seat.

The final two minutes of the game were intense. There were six lead changes. I scored ten points in one minute and 48 seconds… but we lost.

I was devastated. We all were. It was like a bad dream, but I was wide awake.

I didn't cry, but a lot of the guys did. That day, I learned that it's okay to show emotion, but I had been through so much in the last week that the loss didn't break me.

"You had an incredible game," Mom said softly.

"I could not be more proud, Son," Dad added.

"I don't know," Cadence quipped. "They lost. Could he have played that well?"

It should have been a serious moment. I shouldn't have laughed, but I did.

I wanted to be sad because I thought I should be. I felt that my team deserved a moment of silence because we would never play together again, except I wasn't sad. I was proud of us. We accomplished something no other group of guys had been able to achieve, and that didn't make me sad.

Immediately after the game, I was in complete shock. My heart was in a million pieces all over the court, but I realized we weren't scrubs. We got here, and we held our own.

In the locker room, Coach seemed to mirror my emotions.

"Well, guys, we had a record-breaking season. I'd say that's something to be proud of. We have no reason to hang our heads. We made history, and I couldn't imagine doing it with another group of guys."

He started to get teary. The waterworks started up for me as well.

"I've had the distinct pleasure of coaching some of you gentlemen for the past three years. I'm proud of the young men you've grown to be, and I look forward to following your high school careers. Each and every one of you is special, and I will miss each of you dearly."

At this point, tears were streaming down all our faces. My arm was draped around Jude's shoulder, and Will was resting his elbow on mine.

These were my friends, my brothers. We went to war together, and I was going to miss that.

"We love you, Coach," Kyle said, breaking the silence. "I can speak for everyone when I say thank you for all you've done for us these past couple of years. All I did before basketball was get into trouble. You helped me so much."

"Yeah, Kyle probably would've been in jail if it weren't for you, Coach," Jude said jokingly.

Kyle gave Jude a friendly shove, which pushed Will and me to the ground. Everyone laughed.

"Family on me, family on three," Coached yelled.

We all stood up, put our hands in the middle of the huddle and chanted, "One, two, three, family!"

***

I walked out of the locker room to cheering, clapping, signs, and balloons. The love felt incredible.

Everyone was there. Of course, Mom, Dad, and Cay were there, and so were Dom and Brooke, along with their parents, and Brian was there, too. A few of my aunts, uncles, and cousins were in attendance, and so was an old coach with a man I didn't recognize. And Jenn, Jenn was there, too.

Coach Miles was the first to approach me.

"Great game, Son," he exclaimed.

"Thank you, Coach," I replied as he pulled me in for a hug.

"I'm so proud of how you finished. You fought to the end. A true warrior. This is Coach Evans. He is the head coach at the junior college. He really enjoyed watching you play."

"It's nice to meet you, Sir," I said in my best professional voice.

"It's very nice to meet you, young man," he said, leaving my hand throbbing from a very strong handshake. "I was very impressed with your poise and effort. You have a bright future ahead if you keep that up. I'll be keeping my eye on you."

"Thank you, Sir. I appreciate you coming to see me play."

I didn't have time to process what he said before my cousins attacked me, knocking me to the ground. They roughed me up a bit before helping me to my feet.

Everyone said nice things.

"You played well."

"We're proud of you."

"It's too bad you guys lost."

Dom was as nice as he could be.

"You played alright," he remarked, "but if I were still out there, you guys would've won."

"We never made it to the championship when you were here either," Brian countered.

"No one was talking to you, Brian," Dom snapped.

I laughed. They were a dynamic duo.

"Great game, Hunt," Brian said as he gave me a fist bump.

"Thanks, bro," I replied.

Brooke and Jenn were standing next to each other, though I knew neither of them wanted anything to do with the other.

"Yeah, great game, Daniel," Brooke teased.

I ignored her and, instead, walked to Jenn.

"Thank you so much for coming," I uttered.

"That's what *friends* are for," she announced, pretty much to Brooke.

Brooke rolled her eyes and walked away. I was given a glimpse into my life for the next four years. Fun.

"I'm sorry you guys lost," she expressed. "You know, second place is the first loser."

It was exactly what I would expect her to say.

She smiled innocently, and I realized I was crazy about her.

Although we lost, this moment was kind of perfect. All that was missing was Granma Lou, but I knew she was watching. I knew she was proud.

Chapter Twenty-Two

With the game behind me, I had more time to focus on my schoolwork. Initially, I only cared about my grades because of basketball eligibility, but life truly was easier with good grades, so I decided to keep them up.

Besides, Jenn was something of a warden. She was always badgering me about my grades and not just math. She always had her nose in all of my notebooks.

"That girl is a good influence," Mom once remarked.

I started to blush. I hadn't admitted to anyone that I liked Jenn, not that I was embarrassed, but I was horrible with girls. If Brooke taught me anything, she taught me that girls are complicated, and I'm not good with complicated.

"Mom, can I tell you something, and you promise not to get all Mommy on me?" I quizzed.

"You can talk to me about anything, Hunter," she assured, "but my reactions just kind of come over me. I can't make any promises."

I wasn't exactly pleased with her response, but I was willing to take the risk. She would probably start talking funny and make googly eyes, but I guess that's what moms do.

"I think I like Jenn," I confessed.

"I like her, too," she said coyly.

"Come on, Mom," I said impatiently. "You know what I mean!"

"Okay, okay. I'm sorry. It's not every day that my baby comes to me with such big news!"

I knew it. I knew I should have gone to Dad.

"Do you think she likes you?" she continued.

"She *just* decided to be my friend again. I'm trying to give her a little space."

"Space?" she exclaimed. "You're always talking about her, or you're on the phone with her, or you're texting her. You're with her anytime I pick you up from school... I don't think you know the proper definition of space."

She was right.

After the game, Jenn started hanging out with my friends and me. It started one day when she came to talk to me at lunch. Every day since then, she just seemed to be around more. She had kind of become one of the guys to them, but not to me.

"She likes hanging out with us, and she kind of fits in. I just don't want to be friend-zoned."

"What do you know about the friend zone?" she asked, examining my face for answers.

Honestly, I didn't know anything about it. Brooke explained to me that she had friend-zoned me a few days prior.

I thought it best to confront her about the way she treated Jenn. I planned on ignoring her and just kind of co-existing, but she was always around. So, one day, I came clean to her about everything. She never apologized for calling Jenn names or using me for lunch money, but she did break down how she didn't like me – at all – and that I would never be more than a friend to her.

"You were friend-zoned when we were one," she laughed. I didn't find it funny. "But you are my friend, and I'll try to treat your little friends better, even though they're lame."

She was referring specifically to Jenn. They did not like each other... at all. I didn't understand it, but then again, I don't understand girls.

I knew then and there I did not want to be in the friend zone, wherever it was.

"Not much," I replied to Mom, "but I don't need to know much because I don't ever want to go there."

"Well, I think you should leave it alone." Her response was not what I wanted to hear. "Let it happen organically."

Organically.

Our eggs were organic. I didn't know how to make things organic.

"What does that even mean?" I was confused.

She laughed. Why did everyone find my life so funny?

"Let it happen naturally," she answered. "Don't *do* anything, just be."

It wasn't what I wanted to hear, but I suppose it was simple enough.

Mom was always watching lovey-dovey movies. I thought she would want me to make some grand gesture, buy her flowers and candy, something. Do nothing was not what I expected, but I was good at doing nothing. As a matter of fact, I was a pro at it.

"If you say so," I whined.

That was about a week ago. Since then, I had been trying to be organic, but it's hard to *act* natural. I guess I just had to be myself. Maybe that's what Mom meant.

I mulled over this thought at lunch one day while Jude cracked jokes on one of Jenn's friends.

"You're so short," he quipped. "Snow White confused you for one of her dwarves."

His joke was so corny that I laughed.

"That was bad," Jenn remarked. "I know you can do better than that!"

Jude looked her dead in the face and burst out laughing. Everyone joined him, including Jenn. No one knew why we were laughing; we just were.

That was middle school.

Chapter Twenty-Three

Life was pretty good. I had two best friends, my grades were good, and Coach Evans introduced me to a few high school coaches from around the city.

I was happy, and it scared me. Anytime things were going too well, something horrible would happen, stealing the joy right out of my very being. I told Dad my theory, and, as always, he turned it into a lesson.

"Son," he started. "Life is like a game of baseball. When you're at bat, the pitches will try to confuse you. They'll fake you out, and sometimes, they'll even hit you."

"Dad, what are you talking about?" I moaned.

"Stay with me here. In baseball, you get three strikes before you're out, and there are nine innings."

I sighed and slumped into a chair. This was going to take a while.

"Consider this," he continued, sensing my restlessness. "Things won't always go the way you want. You'll get hit with curveballs and strikeout, or you might hit a foul ball, but you have nine innings to make it right. You'll get on base a lot, and every now and then, you'll hit a home run."

I understood where he was going, but I didn't understand why he used sports to explain everything.

"Dad, no sports, please," I pleaded.

"It's simple. Life has twists and turns, like a racetrack."

"Dad!" I cried.

"Sheesh. Okay, okay. Life is tough, you'll get somethings right, and you'll mess up. The important thing is to stay positive and keep trying. Always get back on the horse – I mean – it's not over 'til the fat lady sings?"

By the end, he was unsure of himself, but I understood.

"But why is it always something new?" I asked. "Why is it that when things are going so well, I always get let down?"

"If you look for trouble, you'll find it. Don't speak that into your life. Stay positive. Say positive things, and you'll find positivity in everything you do."

"Kind of like when I'm at the free-throw line, and I think, 'I'm going to miss this,' and I do?"

Dad laughed, "Now who's using sports analogies?"

"Yeah, yeah," I smiled.

"Just stay positive, Son. Don't imagine all the bad things that can happen. Think of all the good. There's so much good in the world. Be that."

He nodded his head. Content with his response, he turned back to the television. He would soon fall asleep with the remote in his hand. He always did. He was so predictable.

I stood up, gave him a pat on the back, and ran up the stairs.

"Stop running in the house," Mom screamed from downstairs.

"Yeah," Cadence added. "You almost knocked my dollhouse over. Who would've cleaned that up? You!"

"No one was talking to you, Cadence," I teased.

She poked her head out of her room and stuck her tongue out at me. I returned the gesture, putting my thumbs in my ears and wiggling my fingers at her. She crossed her arms across her chest and stomped off, rolling her eyes.

My little monster.

I walked into her room and fondly declared, "I love you, Cadence Louise."

She stopped playing with her dolls, looked up at me, and smiled. It warmed my whole heart.

***

Bucket Bros was booming. Initially, I was wary of continuing with Jude, but he promised he would never post anything before I had a chance to watch it. That didn't mean he wouldn't play jokes on me, and I was okay with that.

We had over 100 subscribers and were still growing.

Dom and Brian came on for a guest post, which was pretty cool. Brian and Brooke weren't dating anymore. It was really bothering Dom, and Brian didn't want to do anything to mess up their friendship. See, that's a nice guy.

Meanwhile, my best friends fought all day long. Jude cracked jokes on Jenn, and Jenn made him look dumb. It was fun to watch.

Being Jenn's friend was fine with me. We'd been through a lot. I was thankful that she was my friend at all, and she was the best kind of friend – different than Jude and more like Granma Lou. She was funny and everything, but she cared. She always tried to make sure I was okay.

Mom was right. She was a good influence.

I think Granma would've liked her.

I sat on the couch, and Callie tried to jump onto my lap. She forgot she was old as dirt. I petted her as she fell asleep. It was 9:30. I fought to go to bed at 11 p.m., and there I was, dozing off.

I struggled to keep my eyes open, but sleep won.

I was dead to the world for about 30 minutes until I smelled something funny… in my lap.

"Mom!"

Chapter Twenty-Four

I woke up the next morning in a great mood. Everything was right in the world. My family was good, my friends were great, and it was another bright, sun-shiny day.

Only it wasn't.

It was an ugly day. The sun was not shining. It was overcast and hazy. I peeked through my curtains and caught a glimpse of the sun, but it was covered by clouds, familiar clouds.

I jumped out of bed and ran downstairs. Mom was in the freezer, selecting pre-frozen meals. That could only mean one thing: Dad was leaving. She turned around to my concerned face, and hers softened.

"You saw the flaming clouds?" she asked.

When I was five, Dad did his best to help me understand fire safety and the importance of his job.

"Hunter," he enunciated clearly, "Fires are extremely dangerous. It's important to stay away from fire and smoke."

He showed me a fire extinguisher and explained they were carefully placed around the house.

"Fire tingwisher?" I questioned.

Both he and my mom laughed.

"Yes, Son, 'tingwishers' could be the difference between life and death."

I must have looked a bit scared and confused because my mother gently placed her hand on his shoulder and continued. "As your father said, fires are very dangerous, and his job is to fight them and save people."

"Like a superhero?!" I marveled.

"Yes, Son," Dad acknowledged, sticking his chest in the air. "I'm a superhero, aren't I?"

Mom rolled her eyes.

I jumped into my dad's strong arms, and he flew me around the room, further explaining fire safety and the signs of fire.

"Are clouds smoke?" I probed.

"That's a good question," he beamed proudly. "Some clouds are formed from the smoke. They're called flammagenitus clouds. Any time you see those clouds, there is a fire somewhere underneath, and your dad has to go to work."

"I see flame clouds. Daddy has to go to work," I repeated. "Daddy is a superhero. He has to save people."

Satisfied I understood, Dad put me on his shoulder and reached for Cadence. She was just a tiny baby with huge, curious eyes.

"One day, I'll need you to help your sister understand the importance of fire safety. Can you do that for me?"

"Yes, Daddy. I help Kay-nance."

It was a long time ago, but I remembered that day clearly. I always looked for flame clouds.

Mom packed the freezer bag, which meant Dad wasn't going to the station. He was going straight to the fire.

"Where is it?" I investigated.

"I don't know anything. He just asked me to pack a freezer bag."

"How bad is it?"

"I don't know."

"How many other Jakes have gone?"

She stopped and stared at me inquisitively.

"Do your ears work?" she quizzed.

"Yes," I answered, confused.

"Did you hear me say I don't know anything?"

I hadn't heard her. Big fires always made me nervous.

Sensing my uneasiness, Mom stepped in. "Dad will be fine. He's been called on tougher jobs."

We had picked up a lot of firehouse slang over the years. A job was a fire. My nerves were quieted, knowing he had conquered bigger fires.

"Where is he?" I asked, searching all of downstairs.

"Probably on the toilet," Mom laughed.

Ahh, yes, his throne. I walked up the stairs toward their bedroom.

"You really are a superhero," I heard Cadence announce as Dad backed out of her room.

"I love you, Duchess of Stevenstown," he said as he mockingly took a bow.

He was always willing to play all her make-believe princess games.

"Hey, Hunt," he called. "I was just on my way to your room."

"I saw the flame clouds," I replied.

"So, you know the drill."

"Yes, sir."

"You're the man of the house. Protect the queen and duchess."

He stayed in character for Cadence's sake.

"I shall oblige, my king," I answered with a bow of my own.

He bowed lower. Not to be outdone, I bowed even lower. He started to bow again, only to realize he'd never be able to get as low as me.

"Alright, young legs," he surrendered. "You win. Be good and listen to your mother. I'll text you tonight. Love you."

"Okay, Pops," I returned.

"And?" he asked impatiently.

"And… you be safe out there," I responded, shooting finger guns at him.

He stared me down without blinking.

"I love you, too," I mumbled.

He pulled me into his chest before heading downstairs. After saying a few words to my mom, he was out the door.

I crawled back into bed. It was Saturday. I planned on sleeping the entire day away – and I did.

I woke up at 2:00 p.m. and asked if I could go to Jude's. We had a basketball tournament coming up, and we were going to work on our game.

When I got to Jude's, he was playing a racing game, so I hopped on the sticks.

We never made it to the gym. We played video games until 8:00 p.m.

I called and asked Mom if I could stay the night at Jude's. I ran the risk of rejection with church being early the next morning. She reluctantly agreed, reminding me five times to be home before church the next morning.

I immediately set a reminder on my phone. I didn't want to provide any ammo in the war against my social life. I'd be up and at 'em as early as possible.

Jude made faces as my mom forced me to say, "I love you."

What was up with my parents and expressing their love. You love me, I get it. Can I go now?

As soon as Mom released me from the longest phone call ever, we went outside and played H-O-R-S-E. I won. Honestly, I'm a better basketball player than Jude, but he's a better programmer.

Staying the night at Jude's turned out to be an excellent decision. His house was much more fun than mine. Instead of Mom's boring pot roast, his dad made cheeseburgers on the grill. They were so good. I ate three!

After stuffing our faces, Jude and I played more video games and eventually passed out around 1 a.m.

I was awakened by my phone blaring early in the morning. I reached for the illuminated box in the darkness.

"Hello," I whispered. Jude was still asleep. I didn't want to wake him.

"I didn't forget about church," I lied. "I was just getting up."

Another lie.

"What time is it?" I asked as my eyes adjusted to the light.

5:27 a.m.

"Hunter, I'm coming to get you," Mom stated calmly.

It was too early for church.

"It's okay, Mom. I promise I'll be home before church. Don't worry."

"It's not church."

"I know, I have time," I stammered. I was still asleep, so I wasn't really paying attention to what she was saying... that didn't last long.

"Hunter, it's your father."

I sprung up, ran downstairs, hopped on my bike, and rode like a madman.

There was a thief among us, a terrorist threatening my family. I knew that fire stole from others, that it ruined homes and families. Now it was coming for us.

I needed to get to the castle.

I needed to get to the queen and duchess.

I needed to be a superhero.

Keep reading for an excerpt from
Hunter's next project,
"Project Nimrod: Dazed and Confused,"
coming soon!

I didn't know what was going on, but something had been very weird with Jenn. She was hanging out with "the guys" less, and she had stopped coming to study hall. I thought it might be a girl thing, so I gave her a pass, but when I saw her laughing with Brooke in the hallway, I knew something was wrong.

"Hey, Jenn," I called to her.

She looked at me, giggled a bit, and turned back to B.

Something was definitely going on, and I didn't like it at all.

I didn't want anything major, Cadence's birthday was coming up and Mom wanted to know if Jenn was coming to the party. Since she had gotten so close to my family, I figured she would definitely be there, but who knew what this knew Jenn was thinking.

I turned away, completely perplexed. I wasn't ready to navigate new waters with girls. I just learned how to be friends with one!

Mom once warned me that my female friendships would be different from my relationships with my boys.

"Girls don't care about all of the same things boys do," she schooled, "and their emotions are different."

She was right. Jenn didn't like video games, and she wasn't particularly fond of basketball, but we still had lots in common. We told each other just about everything. That's why this was so confusing. What could she possibly have to talk to Brooke about? They had been sworn enemies for months.

I shook my head and walked away, deciding not to involve myself in girls' business. I would never understand them. It was as if I was willingly walking into a headache.

Nope. Not today.

I walked off in search of Jude or Will. I needed some time with my boys.

I couldn't have gotten more than six steps before Brooke brushed past me, purposely bumping my shoulder. What was going on with these girls?

I looked around, thinking Jenn would be right behind her, but she was nowhere in sight.

Instead, I saw a small piece of folded paper fall to the floor. I almost ignored it, but it had my name on it.

Hunter, it read in the fanciest handwriting I had ever seen.

I picked it up and examined it a bit, it looked like a love letter. Wait... a love letter, from Brooke?

I shoved it in my pocket and ran to the cafeteria as fast as I could. I would definitely need my boys for this!